EN
VACANCES

En Vacances

by

David A. Sutton

Black Shuck Books
www.BlackShuckBooks.co.uk

Versions of the following stories previously appeared as follows:
'Those of Rhenea' in *Skeleton Crew #2* (1988)
'Dead Water' in *The Fourth Black Book of Horror* (Mortbury Press, 2009)
'Tomb of the Janissaries' in *Beneath the Ground* (The Alchemy Press, 2003)
'The Holidaymakers' in *Clinically Dead & Other Tales of the Supernatural* (Crowswing Books, 2006)
'The Dew Shadows' in *A Ghosts & Scholars Book of Folk Horror* (Sarob Press, 2018)

Cover design & internal layout © WHITEspace 2020
www.white-space.uk

First published in the UK by Black Shuck Books, 2020

978-1-913038-56-4

For Anna Taborska

Sant-Agnello, Campania, Italy

It was in the back streets of Sant' Agnello that Matthew first saw what he and Joan would later call the 'cat house'. Or rather, the visible part of the roof of the cat house that could be seen from their fourth-floor room at the hotel Piramide. From ground level the building would have shown no indication that cats lived there. The couple's room at the rear of the hotel overlooked a narrow, twisting alleyway, at the other side of which was a large old building, perhaps a former palazzo, surrounded at its rear by an overgrown garden. The building was comprised of a three or four storey tower directly opposite at one end and a lower, flat-roofed area, with a retaining balustrade at the far end. It was upon this roof they observed several, running to many, cats, roaming about or sunning themselves.

"Perhaps," Joan said between a fork full of linguine, "they're rescue cats..."

"Mangy enough to be, I'd agree." Matthew struggled with his pasta, distracted. He couldn't blame the strays for feeling strange. In fact, both he and Joan had sensed something not quite right – the holiday destination did not seem altogether wholesome or convivial. The gloomy hotel and distant staff didn't help.

He looked up across the hotel restaurant and sighed as he watched the waiter, walking ahead of their dining companions, towards their table. They'd discovered they had to sit at a designated table for their meals and both he and Joan found it somewhat uncomfortable. Whoever else was seated at the same table-for-four would be with you at breakfast and dinner for the whole holiday, like it or lump it.

Joan hadn't noticed the Scottish couple arriving from behind her. "It'll be a charity – cats' rescue. Like our 'Cats Protection'. Oh, hi, both," she said to the couple, with a suppressed sigh, as they sidled up, behind Giulio, the waiter.

Giulio pulled out the chairs and seated the

couple opposite. Matthew was grateful at least that both he and Joan had had half an hour to themselves, before the others arrived.

"I'm nay fond o' cats," Morag said, insinuating herself into the conversation she had overheard. She was from Aberdeen, Matthew recalled, and John was an Orkney-man; both were retired. "Fell beasties and bad luck," Morag scowled. Matthew watched Morag's face scrunch up. She looked like a cat with constipation, he thought. She had a round, flattened face, and the trace of a whisker or two above her upper lip.

The couple were about ten years' senior to Matthew and Joan, and Morag was, in Scottish parlance, a 'dour type'. He found it difficult to converse with them. They had little in common and Morag, in particular, was one of those tourists – everyone meets at least one on holiday – who disliked being abroad, had an aversion to eating 'foreign' food and disparaged being shown around the tourist sites by tour guides speaking in 'broken English'.

John, they had found out, had chosen Sorrento for their holiday as he wished to visit Monte Cassino. He'd served in the army during the famous 1944 battle. The single, tenuous point of context that Matthew felt he could chat about was his manager's war service. His boss had been an artillery tractor driver at the Anzio landings, which preceded Monte Cassino.

"You'll no catch me strokin' one," John added, bringing Matthew out of his reverie. "The hairs y'see." His face was florid enough to suggest he might be allergic to animal fur. As he was handed a menu by the waiter, Morag was already poring over hers and tsk-tsk-ing.

"It'll ha' t'be the grilled chicken again. I'll start with the soup," she barely raised her head from the card.

Joan sipped her Asti and carefully replaced the glass next to her bowl of pasta. "I think it must be good luck that these cats *have* been rescued, you see so many strays over here."

"It's t'be hoped they're nay in the hotel," Morag growled. "Clatty offspring of the sith, as ma granny would say."

"That's 'fairy folk' to you." John translated helpfully. His smile was stiff; evidently he disliked his wife's propensity for gloominess in all things.

Matthew slugged his red wine and refilled his

glass, hoping the effect would render the remainder of the evening bearable.

"In fact," he answered, "you probably won't ever see them. They're... well we think they're trapped... in an old building. On a roof, just not able to get out." He didn't particularly want to explain where they'd seen the cats and the circumstances of their apparent confinement, but felt he had to say something. Matthew stole a glance at Joan – *help me out here* – his eyes flickering the unspoken entreaty.

"The owner," Joan added, "probably has them in quarantine, while the vet treats them. So," Joan turned her head to Matthew as she tried to suppress a smirk, "you won't have to worry about encountering any." Matthew was impressed by Joan's ability to fend off Morag's constant doomy announcements and declarations. But Joan was used to dealing with people, especially complainants, in her job at the Inland Revenue.

Morag's next contribution came out of left field, however, and took Matthew by surprise. "Just as well, just as well." Morag turned to her husband, her brows furrowing, giving him a bizarre look. "We've eno' on our plate with the watchers."

"The watchers?" Joan asked, after a second's hesitation.

"Ay," John responded, "We're being watched, ay."

Both Matthew and Joan gazed at their dining companions nonplussed.

"Ye'll notice soon eno'," Morag spoke in a whisper. "The waiters, the bar staff, ay, and the others on reception... their beady Italian eyes. Always lookin'."

Before any further elucidation could be gained, the odd couple's starters arrived and they began to eat in silence.

~

They finally escaped from the dining room, freshened up, left the hotel and joined the locals in their *passeggiata*, down to the main square and the church of Santi Prisco. The evening was warm, with barely a breath of air, and the locals were out in force, in all their finery. From the wide church steps, the road was bordered on one side by a narrow, cobblestoned pavement, and on the other by a much wider cobbled footpath, with attractive reservations of lawns and flower beds, palms and other trees.

"I feel a bit under-dressed." Joan stared at the crowds and then at her crumpled cheesecloth blouse and faded jeans.

"Well, we dressed up a bit for dinner, that's enough, surely," Matthew replied uncertainly. His tee-shirt, extolling the virtues of English beer, looked positively alien amongst the local men in their dark jackets and waistcoats. "It's too warm for penguin suits."

"But look at me, compared… I mean, look at the red-head about to walk past us," she whispered behind her hand, "the one in the matching high heels."

"Hmm," Matthew said appreciatively as the young woman shimmied past them through the throng, her dress caressing his legs below his shorts. She did that deliberately, he thought.

"And me in my scruffy trainers."

Matthew was smiling inanely. "What?" Joan asked. "Oh, yeah," she cottoned on, "she wouldn't give you the time of day, sunshine. She'd want somebody clean-shaven for a start. A young Italian man. With style!" Now she smiled. "Let's have a cocktail. I won't be so embarrassed if we're sitting at a café."

They jigsawed their way through the crowds

and found a table outside a small osteria. The waiter appeared almost before they settled their bums on the raffia chairs.

"Buona sera, welcome. Would you like something to drink?" he drawled, his accent heavy. His starched shirt and dickie-bow looked almost as formal as the Italian men in the street.

Matthew ordered for them both and they silently observed the locals parade up and down as they waited. Joan was the first to notice.

"They're—"

"—not interacting," Matthew finished for her. There seemed to be no conversation, or what there was was whispered too low to hear. The Italians were sauntering casually, moving and hardly stopping to chat. It was like a slow-motion dance without music, the pace languid. The sky was darkening and the air heavy and moistly warm.

Joan thought the parade of locals was almost funereal. She was about to say as much to Matthew when she felt light-headed. Her eyes drooped as if a wave of tiredness was stealing over her.

Looking at the door to the café Matthew noticed an advertising poster pasted on the glass panel and he idly read out the printed words in his head. 'Notte del Festival – 7 Giugno, Sant' Agnello – Fantasmi e Antichi Dei'. Today's date, he realised. He wondered idly whether the way the locals were promenading wasn't something to do with that, the ghosts and something or other festival.

Joan opened her mouth to say something else when the waiter returned with their drinks and placed a bill in a little shot glass on the table.

"Please. Would signora like something to eat?" He produced a small menu card.

"No, grazie. We have already had something." Joan watched as the waiter nodded and withdrew into the darkened interior of the café, then his face loomed at the window. He appeared to be looking directly at them.

"Does he think we aren't going to pay the bill?" she said limply. "I think he's staring at us. Don't look. Make it casual." It was an effort for her to speak.

Matthew fought the urge to do exactly what Joan didn't want him to. He sipped his brandy.

"I'll stand up to get my wallet," Matthew explained. As he did so he turned slightly to face the frontage of the osteria and saw a man's face withdrawing into the gloom.

"Well, I saw something," Matthew said as he sat back down. "Maybe he's just looking out for customers, although it doesn't appear that the promenaders are interested in giving him their custom."

Joan sipped her limoncello and vodka and they both resumed watching the crowds. They had thinned out somewhat and the road was less busy. But faces that before were fixed ahead were now, from time to time, turned towards the osteria, as if they were trying to keep an eye on the couple, but without making it obvious. The watchers, thought Joan, the odd couple's watchers...

As she gazed sleepily, Joan gasped through her drink. "Look, look, Mat!" She pointed at the piazza in front of the church. "It's the odd couple."

Matthew saw them at once. "He's in his dinner suit..."

"And she's in her bag of a dress."

They watched as the Scottish couple joined the throng of amblers. Pacing along with the same measured steps as the locals.

"It's like they're being drawn in..." Joan added

"And we're the ones being watched..."

Matthew added. Joan shivered at her husband's realisation.

~

After they arrived back at the hotel, they found their room much too warm and so took to the balcony with a bottle of wine. Matthew and Joan tried in vain to count the cats again, trying to take their thoughts off the bizarre passeggiata they had witnessed. In fact there were so many cats, it was simply not possible to definitively count them all; they came and went, presumably entering and leaving by a door or opening at the side of the tower which faced away from their hotel window. The open door was inferred by a rectangle of bright light cascading across the flat roof.

Most of the felines they'd seen earlier in the day would appear and lounge in the sun on the hard stonework of the roof. They were scrawny things, black, tabby, or multi-coloured; strays, as Joan would have it, taken in by the owner of the palazzo. It was Matthew who now noticed the poo and the piddle. The cats, it seemed, were forced to defecate on the very area in which they took their leisure. During the day it must have proliferated, for in the evening light many little dark dollops could be observed, along with damp patches, dotted randomly on the roof.

"At least thirty," Joan was tapping her fingers as she counted.

"Have you noticed the shit?" Matthew screwed up his nose as if he could smell the sour cat pee and poo stench. He refilled his wine glass and drank most of it. "That's *not* the sign of a cat-saviour. More like a dotty old woman who doesn't know when to stop taking in strays, and in any case can't look after them. I've counted at least forty-five."

Joan nodded. "God, that's awful. It must stink to high heaven down there." She came away from the balcony rail and sat next to her husband. "I can still see them through the railings, but I'm not going to look," she said. "It'll put me off the wine."

The cats were beginning to have an extraordinary effect on them both. If at first it was a little Italian mystery, it had now become an unsavory vision. Joan imagined the house overrun with hundreds of strays, not just the few dozen they'd casually counted, each littering the old palazzo floors with their mess. Each individual cat forced to live amongst its own fecal dirt unless it could find its way onto the roof and some small respite from the foul miasma that must have permeated the lower rooms. She sipped her wine, raised her head to the sky and tried to see the stars and, if possible, breathe some fresh, unpolluted air.

"Bloody hell, look at that!" Matthew had stood up and was leaning over the rail, staring at the cat house.

"I don't think I want to, thank you very much."

In spite of herself, she glanced through the railings and nearly dropped her glass. A shiver went through her as if she had been seized on the shoulders by a pair of freezing cold hands.

The cats were sitting on their haunches and were all facing the hotel. In fact, facing *their* balcony. They were motionless. Their heads were raised and their gleaming gold, almost phosphorescent, eyes stared, unblinking.

"They're looking at *us*..." Matthew waved his empty wine glass over the balcony, as if to shoo the cats away or make them jump. But they were too far away for that.

Joan put down her glass and crossed her

arms over her shoulders to stop the shivers. "They must only just have noticed us..." she rationalised, attempting to deflect the cats' bizarre behaviour away from the abnormal. But she couldn't help appreciating the similarity of the watching cats to the watching Italians.

"Their eyes – bloody well reminds me of *The Midwich Cuckoos*."

"Yes, I've only just noticed, they all have the *same* eye colour." Joan slid back the balcony door, intending to retreat inside. "It's like we're prey and they're watching us to see our next move. Anyway, I'm starting to cool off." The sound of her voice, she thought, was as if spoken by someone else, as if the cats had somehow hypnotized her.

"Just normal cat behavior, then," Matthew quipped, thinking their behavior was anything but normal. He followed Joan into their room, switching off the balcony light. In the gloom outside the cats' eyes glowed, floating pairs of unblinking gold irises and black-slit pupils.

"Close the curtain, Mat," Joan said. "Then they can't see us." She shook her head, trying to jettison her sensation of dislocation.

~

The next morning, the cat poo was gone and so were the cats, the roof uniformly wet.

"They've hosed it all away," Joan called from the open window. "Come and look."

Matthew put his head out and nodded a confirmation. "You're right, the roof is wet. And the cats have gone." As he returned to the bathroom he added, "I wonder why they don't let the cats out into the garden? It'd be far less messy." He was trying to forget the bizarre way the animals had acted.

Yesterday they hadn't noticed any cats in the parts of the garden they could see from their balcony. "I imagine she might get complaints from the neighbours if she allowed hundreds of cats to roam free..."

"She?"

Joan hesitated. "Well, isn't it more likely that it would be a she who takes in stray cats, rather than a he?" It was perhaps a stereotypical assumption.

"Anyway, whatever, what's on the agenda for today? Breakfast and then down to the town and the beach?"

"I'd like to take a trip into Naples, actually." She looked at her watch. "Still a bit early for breakfast anyway." Shopping in a busy city would, she expected, lighten her mood.

"Well, we could—"

"Forget it superman, I've just had a shower."

"No, what I was going to say was, how about we have a little stroll and check out the cat house?"

Joan felt the shiver on her shoulders again. "Check out? What's to check? I think I might have had enough of those crazy cats." She decided she might be reluctant to use their balcony for late night drinks again during the rest of their holiday. To avoid being watched by the cats.

"We'll just toddle around to the back of the hotel and take a look from ground level."

"To see what? We're certainly not going to knock on the door and make enquiries as to the welfare of the house's cats." But she acquiesced. "But I'm happy to have a walk before we face the odd couple at breakfast!"

Matthew laughed. "But maybe not as odd as those moggies!"

Finding their way to the narrow, cobbled passageway that their hotel room overlooked was not as straightforward as it at first appeared. They exited the hotel arm in arm and turned right onto the road that ran alongside the hotel's palm-fringed garden. Matthew had assumed that it would be a straightforward process to walk along and find the cobbled street which should run off the main road down the rear of the building. But they passed it and continued on with no side roads in evidence for quite a few hundred yards.

They then came to a turning on the right – not the cobblestone alleyway, but a road. "Let's turn here and see where it takes us," Matthew suggested. The side road was quieter, and soon the traffic noise and the snarl of motor scooters was fading. The tree-lined avenue was very pleasant, with smart, two storey houses with ornate wrought iron gates leading to manicured front gardens. The houses had colonnades in the classical style, with balconies, pediments and red tiled roofs. Others were simpler, plainly walled dwellings, nicely painted and with trim shuttered windows.

"I think," Matthew said, "that if we go much further, we'll end up in the sea."

"Maybe not, Mat." Joan swerved to the right, dragging Matthew with her. Almost hidden by a festoon of road furniture advertising hotels and retail shops towards the coast, plus a no-entry sign for vehicles, was a narrow alleyway, paved with brick cobbles.

As they walked along, the rear of buildings backed onto the passageway, windowless and with flaking paint peeling from the surfaces, run down in contrast to the previous road's dwellings. "Back home they'd have called this a gulley or a ginnel in the north," Joan commented.

"Well, the Romans didn't build this one," Matthew remarked as they walked, weaving right and left as the little pathway meandered in every direction. Then, as they turned a sharp corner, Matthew saw their hotel backing onto the alleyway, and their balcony hovering above its counterparts on the lower floors. "We're here. Look, there's my beach towel hanging over the rail."

Both of them turned about and saw the old palazzo from the ground up for the first time. The plain walls of the alleyway's faceless buildings were finally broken by a rusty iron gate, overgrown with vines.

"Through there must be the garden," Joan said.

Matthew walked over and peered through the greenery. "Can't see much, other than it's completely overgrown." They walked on a few yards, the walls of the cat house as equally cracked and flaking as the alley's other buildings.

"And that's the tower," Joan said looking upwards. "Oh, and here's the door." The higher part of the building rose up with two shuttered windows designating the floor levels.

The wooden door was set into an archway, and was ornately heavy, with faded, flaking blue paint. A single bronze coloured ring acted as door handle and presumably knocker. There was no letterbox. A film of dust coated the door.

"And, look, up there," Joan pointed to the right. "The flat roof where we see the moggies." The ornate old balustrade that hemmed in the cats was unmistakable.

Matthew was a tad disappointed. What they had thought to be an old palazzo was little more than an old, run-down town house in need of some considerable renovation. Then he noticed something on the arched stone transom above the door. He thought at first it was the name of the dwelling chiseled into the stone, obscured by dirt and weathering.

"It says something..." He approached the door and raised his hands, just managing to reach the stonework, rubbing at the lettering.

"It's in Italian," Joan said irrelevantly.

"Well spotted Doctor Watson!" Matthew stepped back in a cloud of dust, coughing.

"It says," Joan screwed up her eyes and stood on tip-toe to read, "Museo... dei Gatti... Mummificati. That's—"

Matthew interrupted in astonished tones, "Well, the museum of mummified cats! Jesus, do you think—" He dismissed the thought before he expressed the notion that anyone would be disposing of strays and then mummifying them.

Joan took an even stronger dislike to the house than before, and suddenly wanted to be anywhere else. "It's giving me the creeps already. Let's get back, Mat."

Matthew was about to demur, but the look on his wife's face convinced him to change his mind. But he was thinking that it made for a peculiar, maybe very peculiar, coincidence. The house was a museum as stated above the door, or rather probably had been but was no longer open for business, and now it was a home for living cats, instead of dead ones.

The shopping trip to Naples took Joan's mind off the cat house, but it had been an exhausting day.

"I think I'm ready for bed," she called out, towelling her hair as she came out of the bathroom. She felt fatigue of a sort, but aided and abetted by an unusual dizzy somnolence.

Matthew was leafing through some brochures in the hotel's guest information folder, thinking that he was pretty tired too. "We will, Joany, but dinner's at eight... We'll have an early night right after." He glanced at his watch. "As soon as we can escape the odd couple!"

Joan visibly withered. "Fuck." She began putting on the dark blue dress that Matthew liked; it fitted her lithe figure perfectly. He had already dressed in a crisply ironed, short-sleeved shirt and tan trousers. Although not too formal, the hotel expected the 'smart casual' rule to be maintained.

On the balcony, a breeze was cooling their over-hot room. Matthew stepped outside, intending to see the state of play at the cat house. Instead his eyes were drawn directly down to street level when movement caught the periphery of his vision.

The alleyway was in partial darkness, as there were no streetlamps and sunset was fast approaching. Matthew watched as two people walked arm-in-arm hesitantly along the path. He could see by their gait that they were having trouble negotiating the rough, uneven stones of the passageway.

"Well, I'll be blowed... come and look at this."

"I really don't want to see those bloody cats again," Joan answered, an icy shiver passing through her.

"No, it's the odd couple. Down there." The two people had nearly reached the door of the cat house. They were treading slowly, very carefully, almost as if they were sleepwalking.

"Well let's hope," Joan replied maliciously, "that they get completely lost and miss dinner." She paused to apply lipstick in front of the dressing table mirror. "C'mon, I'm ready."

Joan's hope was realised as, after half an hour had elapsed, the Scottish couple had not materialised at the dining table.

When the waiter arrived with their starters,

Matthew asked, "Giulio, do you know if the other couple are joining us for dinner?"

"I don' think so Mister Matthew. I think they are, how you say, indispose'."

"They're not well?" Joan queried. "We saw them. No, well Matthew saw them outside, at the back of the hotel…"

"I could've been mistaken," Matthew said to Joan hurriedly, willing to admit a misperception. To the waiter he asked, "Did they say they were poorly?" Considering it was a blessing not to have them at the dining table, Matthew wondered why he and Joan were taking such an unwarranted amount of interest in their welfare.

"Maybe they drink something they didn' like," Giulio offered, presenting his open palms and hunching his shoulders dismissively, as if further queries would be impossible to answer.

What a funny thing to say, Joan thought. When the waiter had gone, she said, "Did he mean to suggest they were drunk?"

"Drunk?"

"You know, as in pissed as newts and can't walk in a straight line to the dining room." She negotiated a piece of pastrami around her plate with her fork, not feeling particularly hungry.

"Well, they were walking rather strangely, as far as I could see – if it was them. Very hesitantly. It was getting dark and I thought they were being careful not to trip over."

Joan waved her fork at her husband and grinned, as if to indicate that *there* was the answer. Then she thought about it. "Mind you, I don't recall them having anything but water at the table. Out-and-out teetotallers…"

"Do you think we should go and have a look?"

"Don't even think about it! Early night, remember? And it might not have been the odd couple, you said yourself you could have made a mistake."

"Not even to go out for the passeggiata?" Matthew smiled.

"That would be too creepy by half." Joan had convinced herself that it was safest to stay in the hotel now, except when going to the beach or into town.

~

The balcony door was open, but Joan had pulled the curtain across. Fresh air could circulate, she thought, but leave temptation to go out there screened off. She settled her head on the pillow and waited for Matthew to relax in his adjacent bed. Her eyes were heavy-lidded, thoughts muted to a hypnotic fog.

Matthew was tempted to take a peek over the balcony but knew that Joan would be upset if he did. As he undressed, he speculated on the odd couple. Had he really seen them in the alleyway, or was it two other people who looked similar? It had been quite dark and he could have been mistaken. But then, why hadn't they come down for dinner? Their waiter had said they were indisposed, so *he* knew they would not be dining. Nothing sinister in that. He slipped beneath the sheets and turned to face Joan. She made a quiet sound, her breathing measured in slumber.

Switching off the light between the beds, he tried to relax.

It was that uncertainty about whether he was awake or dreaming that brought him, rising, up out of the dark pit of sleep, breathless from the smell of unclean cats. Had he heard the wail of a cat? Or was it just that the likeness of a mummified cat lingered like a fading after-image at the back of his eyes? All tattered yellow-grey wrappings around a legless, vaguely cat-shaped body, decaying slowly within its covering.

Lying in the darkness Matthew stilled his breath to listen. The wooden curtain rings were clicking on their rail as the heavy curtain was caught in a stray breeze. Then he heard them. Definitely felines. Wailing somewhere in the distance. They chilled Matthew's blood with their human baby-like cries.

He turned to see if they had woken Joan, but she was seemingly breathing quietly, undisturbed. Cautiously, he drew back the sheet and, without switching on the light, slipped out of bed, then shuffled out onto the balcony, careful not to make the curtain rings clatter.

There was hardly a stray beam of light, except from a room across and below theirs, and the alleyway below and much of the cat house was in total darkness. The roof where the cats roamed was, however, lit a pale yellow by light from the hotel bedroom below. The stone balustrade around the flat roof was highlighted and the shaped gaps between the balusters cast elongated, strangely cat-shaped images upon the roof, which was otherwise uniformly dark.

Matthew leaned over, the wind coursing between the metal rails of the balcony making the hairs on his bare legs stand up. There was another cat cry and he turned his head this way and that to identify where the sound was coming from. Movement on the cat house roof caught his attention. There was something there, moving among the dark shadows. He strained his eyes to see, although no doubt it was just one of the cats roaming its domain, perhaps calling for a mate.

Then someone, one of the other hotel guests, switched on a light in one of the bedrooms below. And as more gleams penetrated the gloom Matthew was able to discern further. On the roof there was someone standing, a diminutive figure... Matthew drew in a breath and quickly backed away from the rail. The figure was a cat, staring with its gold eyes in his direction. That was bad enough, but...

It was also standing, totally motionless, on its *hind* legs.

Matthew reached for his phone and turned on the assistance light, intending to prove or disprove the bizarre phenomenon of a cat in such a human-like posture. The beam penetrated the blackness, but its glare was too diffused to illuminate the cat house roof. Instead it picked up movement in the alley below.

Matthew leaned over the rail again and watched as a ghostly figure glided over the cobbles heading for the museum's doorway. It took a few seconds for him to realise that what he was seeing from directly above was a naked woman. She was treading cautiously, bare-footed; her blond hair reminded him of Joan, but of course...

He didn't need to guess that the woman was about to enter the now open museum doorway. When she had disappeared, walking zombie-like – in fact somewhat in the manner of the Italians in their passeggiata – Matthew withdrew into the bedroom and moved round to the other side of Joan's bed. The bedsheets were casually awry and he saw that both pillows had been slung beneath them. It took a few shocked seconds for Matthew to realise what was going on. He dashed on a pair of shorts, a shirt and flip flops, and flew down the corridor for the hotel lift.

Almost in a daze of horror he reached the alleyway at the back of the hotel. Only as he approached the ancient doorway did he realise that he had been running in darkness, oblivious of the hazards underfoot, and had forgotten to bring his phone.

Joan had somehow been drawn to the place, had been hypnotised, drugged, kidnapped. His thoughts were wavering, flying in all directions to attempt to account for the circumstances. Yet in his terror he didn't hesitate to fling himself through the aperture of the open door of the museum of mummified cats; adrenaline driving him on without thoughts of any consequence.

He took little heed of his surroundings as he plunged over slippery tiles in almost total darkness.

His headlong flight brought him into a large room with an insipidly gloomy chandelier lighting the space below.

Matthew halted and through tearful eyes saw that he had entered the mummified cat exhibition. Around about the walls, below narrow windows, were glass cabinets of different sizes, dusty with grime. Almost without volition he found himself tiptoeing along the exhibits, peering through the smeared glazing. In the cases were many varied mummified felines, some as if standing, displaying their legs and tails, others wrapped tight, creepily like little human babies. All were in different states of preservation, some consisting of mere skin and bone, their limbs almost bat-like with stretched skin between ribs. One displayed a terrifying screaming skull, jaw agape, teeth sharply defined. Others stood wrapped, with sewn-on beady eyes vaguely reminiscent of the cats on the roof.

Of all the objects in the chamber, one dominated. It was a room-tall statue, a shapely female form with the head of a cat, black in colour, with long, upright, pointed ears. The body was decorated with gold strips, and around its neck was a wide gold and jewel-encrusted necklace. On a raised dais before it, a human-shaped figure lay, covered with a black cloth.

Matthew was taking all this in when Joan appeared out of the darkness beyond the statue.

"Here is our lady of slaughter, Matthew." She gestured with her naked arm. She recognised him, but her eyes were glazed over.

"Joan!"

"Daughter of Ra and Isis."

Matthew strode purposefully up to his wife and gripped her arms with his ice-cold hands. "Joan, you're fucking *naked!* Did you walk out of the hotel like that? What the hell d'you think you're doing!"

Joan stared ahead, not seeing Matthew, totally hypnotised.

"For god's sake, Joany, snap out of it... Here, wrap my shirt around you and we can go back..." He shook Joan viciously, back and forth.

Realisation dawned then. He wasn't meant to be here. Joan had left her pillows in her bed to fool him. The ritual, whatever it was, was not meant for his eyes. Joan had been selected to perform some kind of devilish rite and he should have been fast asleep in bed.

Behind the statue, low down, pinpricks of light emerged, turned into gold phosphorescent eyes. Above them in the deeper darkness, shuffling human shapes; perhaps that was the odd couple amongst them... Matthew watched as the woman they'd previously seen, the one in the red shoes, emerged into the wan light. Her face displayed a puzzled expression, not expecting Matthew at the ritual.

"Le figlie di Bastet uccideranno i nemici di Ra," she intoned. "Bastet's daughters will murder Ra's enemies."

She was wearing a black cape with a hood and some kind of Egyptian inspired amulet around her neck, but lacked any other clothing.

"I don't—" Matthew's words were cut short as he felt something cold at the side of his neck.

Joan had raised her hands and shrugged off Matthew's grip on her elbows. Her left hand caressed his head and held it tenderly, and he thought *thank God, she's waking up*. Then her right hand quickly flicked away and back again, and a glint of silver light reflected from the gloom and into the corner of Matthew's eyes.

This time the sensation in his neck was more pronounced, a singularly sudden pain. He raised his hand to find liquid gushing from the slippery fold of flesh that had opened above the collar of his shirt.

The sound of splashing on the tiled floor heralded sudden dizziness, a haziness, a fog that smeared Joan's statue-like features before him. Matthew reached out a hand, sticky with gore, towards her. He was unable to speak, his throat choked with foam and blood. He wanted to say *I love you* and he guessed that she understood the unspoken sentiment. Though she didn't acknowledge him.

But at least she smiled.

Delos, Cyclades archipelago, Greece

Except when she thought about it, the frenzy of Athens was a million miles away. When she did, flashes of its uncontrolled lifestyle tore through Elizabeth's brain like an express train.

The recent elections had daubed the city with myriad banners, hung between every available lamp post and tree, or across buildings, advocating this party or the other. The equally strident calls to the faithful from the various political headquarters in Ormonia Square – their loudspeakers issuing the usual pre-election promises interspersed with Greek muzak at an ear-stinging rate of decibels – were guaranteed to inflame the heart of any Hawkwind fan. If it wasn't the noise of the political canvassing, to which you were even at risk on the trolley buses, from leafleteers, it was the incessant roar of traffic.

Elizabeth's hotel, the Alexandros, was just off Vas Sofias, up by the American Embassy, and the noise from the omnipresent automobiles and their obligatory horns had, in the end, become almost restful. Twenty-four hours a day Athens is penetrated, she thought, like some symbolic vagina, by motor cars driving across the city at dizzying speeds. By night and the streetlamps, the polluting fog of carbon monoxide fumes lay like a thick pale-yellow duvet over the lower parts of the city.

Now though, Athens was a half-remembered dream...

She had met Steve at a bar in Syntagma Square – no emotional entanglement so far, thank God – and they had both found they were going to Naxos in two days' time. Although the largest of the islands in the Cyclades, Naxos had no airport, which Steve had said he found surprising. Elizabeth, not looking forward to it, was initially pleased. However, the ten-hour ferry trip had, been crowded and unpleasant, with an unhelpful Greek crew. Only the barman made any attempt at friendliness and Elizabeth had been glad of Steve's company.

From the Venetian charm of Naxos town – it seemed that every Greek island had at one time bent to the maritime will of the great Italian empire – Steve persuaded Elizabeth to join him on a boat trip to the fabled island of Delos.

Steve had won her over with his surprised looking, but attractive, crew cut, his cheap black plastic sunglasses and the freckles that appeared to form a halo on his skin around them, and his anecdotes from Greek Mythology. He was on sabbatical from Boston University and had plenty of time for travel, and he seemed to like to keep moving, even when he was staying in one place. She'd have been just as happy to stay on the beaches soaking up the sun, and Naxos was relaxing, but another boat trip appealed to her, so long as it wasn't as daunting as the crossing from Piraeus.

The only thing which dampened her enthusiasm, albeit briefly, was the curious incident in the National Museum of Antiquities, which had taken place the day before their departure from Athens. The day after she'd met Steve, he took her to lunch and then to the museum. It was a vast, staggering array of treasures and she'd felt dwarfed by the sculpture, the gold, the overwhelming decorative eloquence of Greek history.

For his part, Steve was less interested in the magnificence of Agamemnon's gold death-mask, or the bronze statue of Poseidon, and more inclined to the less dramatic pieces. "Especially those two steatite pyxides." After he'd pointed, Steve helpfully explained that they were trinket boxes, made of soapstone. He lingered long over the cabinet in which they resided along with other, similar artifacts, looking at the items, labelled as having been discovered in a grave on Delos.

"See the carving on those lids?" he said to Elizabeth, who was itching to move on.

"Mmm." She was sure her growing boredom was beginning to show. It was, after all, merely grooves cut or chiselled into the lids of the cylindrical boxes.

"A spiral pattern. Very simple." He paused. What was he trying to say, Elizabeth wondered?

"Very like... *very* like spiral carvings in Britain and Ireland from four-thousand years ago."

"Is there a connection, then?" Elizabeth asked.

"A mystery at least," he replied. "Prehistoric, pagan symbology…"

Elizabeth was about to say something, but noticed that Steve was lost, hypnotised, transfixed by the objects. She stared down at them too, trying to see what it was that he was finding *so* fascinating. Then she was subjected to an optical illusion, or so she thought at first. As when sometimes a particular type of pattern in carpet or wallpaper defies the eye's usual ability to see two-dimensionality, and parts of the design assume a three-dimensional region of space between the observer and the flatness of the motif itself. Shake your head, but it still insists in occupying space where the logical mind tells you it isn't. These coils were doing that to her. She wondered if that was why Steve was particularly taken with them.

She was about to phrase that question when she was overcome by a dizzy spell. The spirals, two maze-like hummocks, swum round making her feel as if she was turning in the opposite direction. A sensation of nausea tensed her stomach. Her legs were beginning to swing clear of the floor. Her arms flailed out to stop the unwanted motion.

"The breasts of the queen of ghosts," a voice spoke, though it did not sound like Steve's. It was harsher, rasping, ugly. The words stole over her emotions, taking on a weight far heavier than the mere syllables themselves.

The voice continued.

"Are they not compelling." It was spoken rhetorically. "The unwary traveller may succumb to her ways."

The malignant voice was gone as suddenly as it had appeared and so too was the illusion. Elizabeth found she was leaning into Steve's supporting arms.

"You all right?" he asked, his eyes expressing concern.

"Hmm. Dizzy, just a dizzy spell. It must be too warm in here."

"Well, let's sit you down for a while, eh?" Steve was leading her by the elbow to a nearby bench.

"No, really, Steve. I feel so silly. I'm okay. Really." Several people were staring and she felt slightly embarrassed. They sat nevertheless and Elizabeth was grateful to be able to feel cool marble walls at her back.

"You look like you're about to ask me a

question?" Steve was rummaging in his bag for the guidebook.

Elizabeth was about to ask him whether the wormy carvings had had a similar hallucinatory effect on him. Instead, she said, "Who, or what, is the 'queen of ghosts'?"

"Quite a question for someone with a professed lack of mythological knowledge." he replied.

She looked at him, smiled sweetly at his expression of mock disdain and said nothing. He finally relented. "She, the queen of ghosts, is Hecate, a minor deity in Greek myth, but she's assumed a wider influence world-wide – darkly associated with the ghastly underworld," he added with an amused, sinister flourish.

"Any connection with those trinket boxes?" Elizabeth found herself asking despite the thought of having to explain to him her auditory hallucination.

"Well, not that I'm aware of... Might be worth a little research though. But—"

Elizabeth knew what was coming and interrupted. "Well, I'm feeling much better now."

"Ok, fancy a trip down Mycenae way? It's the next exhibition room..."

"I'm not too good in the sun," he had said, talking about sunbathing.

Naturally, Elizabeth had thought, his freckled face that had made him so attractive to her in the first place. And that wiry red hair. She also liked the soft New England accent in his voice and his lack of brashness. It was interesting to discover a man less outgoing and more reserved than her, especially in an American. Her own job, in catering, meant she led a busy lifestyle, travelling and talking to clients about menus and venues; preparing the food and presentation with her small staff, and so on. Elizabeth's idea of a holiday, therefore, was to keep off her feet as much as possible.

The boat swayed rhythmically on a calm Aegean Sea. The sensation was hypnotic. Elizabeth relaxed in her bikini on a spare bit of deck, her brown body deliciously warm, and she could almost feel her auburn hair becoming bleached in the hot sun. The mix of voices from the other passengers provided a background drone along with the sputtering of the boat's engines. It was dreamy and pleasurable.

She felt herself drifting off, hypnagogic, aware of a dream she was about to have, a strange encounter on Delos, deep into the phantasmal past when Zeus chained the wandering island to the bottom of the Aegean with adamantine chains.

"Here, hold this," Zeus said, his voice a soft lilt for such a god.

Elizabeth stirred, unwilling to allow the waking dream to finish, but Zeus – no, it was Steve – shook her shoulder. "Don't fall asleep in this sun!"

She opened her soft brown eyes and squinted at him. "I was just about to have a good time with Zeus," she said, smiling. "And don't worry about me – it's you who need to keep out of the sun, Steve."

"Don't bother about that now, here, take hold of this." He handed her his rucksack loaded with camera equipment. "It might slip off the boat." He then turned to the rail and pointed his lens seaward. In the distance were islands; you couldn't escape them in this part of the world, but the tour guide was telling everyone that they could now observe Delos.

"There she blows," Steve puffed as he pushed

his sunglasses back on his head, squinting his pale blue eyes briefly before hiding them behind the camera. Tourists were stirring, their lethargy over as the distant island closed towards them.

The dusky female Greek voice boomed from the loudspeaker once more. "Well ladees and chentlemen, we are nearly at the ancien' islan' of Delos. I hope you will enjoy your afternoon here. Remember, please," she continued while Elizabeth pulled on a pale pink blouse and shorts, "you belonck here only four 'ours and you mus' return back to the boat by four-thirty. Thank you."

Within half an hour they had all disembarked from a small jetty and began to wander slowly inland under the dry, burning sun. Steve was risking his arms, exposed from the sleeves of a tee-shirt, but he wore jeans and hot-looking hiking boots. Elizabeth began to wonder briefly if her flat shoes were the right choice after all, looking at the terrain. Some people, she observed, had gone straight to the small museum to be in the shade or to find refreshments. Delos might well be an unmissable stop for Greek history, but four hours in this heat, with virtually no shade, was almost frightening. The island spread out in front of them as Steve headed for the Agora, the large, worn grey blocks of the old marketplace reminding her that time had stood still here. In the distance the gentle slope of Mount Cynthus rose up out of the small island. Steve's camera began to click, providing a counterpoint to the never-ending rasp of the cicadas hidden in the sparse, sun-bleached grasses that grew between the tumbled blocks of the ruins.

It had been hot in Athens, but this! Elizabeth began to perspire. How did Steve manage in those clothes, and with the rucksack, she asked herself.

Cynthus' domed peak was hazed by the rising heat and it made her think back to that evening, the lovely cool evening on Lykabettos where Steve had taken her after the museum. At night the distant lights of Athens had spread below them, a twinkling, moving wash of jewels. They had drunk some wine at the restaurant and felt the cool breeze while moths flitted around the lamps. And, she thought, they'd gone up Lykabettos hill in the cable car. Mount Cynthus had no such luxury to reach its ancient theatre and sprawling ruins. No cool wind either, but instead an open blue sky through which the sun flared, white-hot.

The heat-haze seemed to be making arabesques in front of Elizabeth before she realised she was walking on the ancient floor of a house, its remarkably preserved mosaic surface portrayed a disturbingly familiar labyrinthine pattern. Steve sat by the remains of a wall and was changing film. "Did you know," he said, "that this place was once the cultural and trading empire of the Greeks?" He clicked the back of the camera shut. "Got it." Elizabeth had heard the tour guide on the boat say as much but knew that Steve probably had even greater knowledge about the island. She sighed. It wasn't that she lacked interest, but the heat...

A lizard, the palest green colour, scuttled across marble walls. Cicadas hummed. Suddenly, she realised that there was no one else, other than Steve, nearby. The harbour was invisible, hidden by the contours of the land. The only sound was the island's primal insect inhabitants. Standing on hot mosaics, between what remained of the walls of what was probably a merchant's house, Elizabeth looked down into a well to see black water deep below, as unmoving as the fugitive shadow she glimpsed within it. Other crumbling buildings surrounded them, with a profusion of tall, yellow grass finding hospitality everywhere.

Steve stood up and began looking at his guidebook. "The French first started excavating here in 1873," he offered. "And it's continued right up to the present day."

"Yes, I know. This place is 'second only to Pompeii for archeological completeness'." Elizabeth quoted. "I heard the guide tell us." The parched grass was so still, like a photograph. Nothing stirred.

"But isn't it magnificent," Steve added, apparently unaware of an atmosphere Elizabeth was too easily detecting. "The shrines and temples and houses of a cosmopolitan city..."

"It's beginning to give me the creeps."

"What?" Click went the shutter. "It's all ruins. There's nobody here except us tourists."

"Where are they then?" she shuddered, despite the burning she felt on her legs. Elizabeth struggled with her thoughts, to find coherence, but the nagging worry didn't surface. "There might be snakes." It was the first thing she could think of saying.

"Well there are supposed to be venomous snakes on some of the islands..." Steve suddenly thought better of continuing. He put his arm round Elizabeth's shoulders and kissed her lightly on the lips. They embraced. It seemed so natural and, Elizabeth conceded, so reassuring. But no emotional entanglements, she reminded herself. She'd probably never see him again after her holiday.

Nevertheless, she found the press of his body against hers comforting amidst those dry, ancient, watchful ruins.

~

Mount Cynthus' human artifacts climbed in front of them. Both Steve and Elizabeth were sweltering, sweating profusely now. The island was spreading out behind and below them, the sea a rich blue, invitingly cool. Steve was running through his films, this time using a zoom lens, back down to the distant architecture of the Terrace of the Lions and the four remaining columns of the Poseidoniasts building. Elizabeth could at last see people, in the distance, like gaily coloured ants crawling about, and behind them the reassuring harbour and the tourist boats, lazily bobbing.

"Those lions used to border a sacred lake which was fed from a spring somewhere on this mountain, if you can call it a mountain." Elizabeth mumbled that she *had* heard as they stumbled on upwards, past the half-moon of the amphitheatre. She could hardly believe there had ever been surface water on such a desiccated island.

"Who was it again," she asked, "that this island was sacred to?"

Steve turned back to face her, his sunglasses a burnished black, hiding his weak eyes. "Delos was the birthplace of Apollo and Artemis – you know, the offspring of Zeus and the mortal, Leto." Then he asked himself, without expecting any answer, "Oh, and wasn't Artemis related in some way to Hecate?"

"God of the Sun and Goddess of the Moon, Apollo and Artemis?"

"Yeah!" He was pleased that at last she seemed to be taking an interest in their expedition.

On a different tack Elizabeth sat and said, "D'you mind if we have a rest, Steve?"

He didn't say anything, but stood wiping the sheen of wet from his reddened brow. They had been on the island for an hour and a half, and to her it had seemed forever. It was a fascinating place, of that there was no doubt, but the sun was merciless and the quiet stillness unnerved Elizabeth. It was so unlike the ruins in Athens, those ponderous columns and temples, full of people, surrounded by the heartening life of the modern city. Here a dreamlike atmosphere washed over her and curious, unsurfaced fears slowly paced the depths of her mind. She had heard of the unseen presences supposed to stalk the island, Steve had told her that. She could believe it.

"Why *did* they take away all the graves?" Elizabeth asked. It was merely one mystery of many, but that thought disturbed her, especially now they had almost become part of Delos. The rest of the four hours might be an eternity.

"In 45 BC Delos was purified and all corpses removed from ground visible from the Sanctuary," Steve recapitulated his Greek history, nodding to the peak of the hill. "Then later all ancient tombs were excavated and removed. Since then," he added, "no births or deaths have been allowed on the island, nobody is allowed to stay permanently."

"And nobody lives here now…"

"They were all taken to Rhenea."

"Who, the inhabitants?" She removed a wet wipe from her bag and breathed a languid sigh as she wiped her face with the cold tissue. Dust scrambled as her foot slid quickly away from an unusually inquisitive lizard. A few forlorn poppies stood out against the stones from whose cracks they grew.

"No," he answered, "the cadavers. They were re-buried over there, behind Hecate's Isle." There was that name again! He pointed to the nearby island which was clearly visible from the hill. It looked much like any small Greek island from where they sat, but Elizabeth thought it would be better not to visit such a place. She hoped that there was not some additional boat trip available to Rhenea. It was unlikely. After all, they'd only two hours left on Delos before their little Greek craft would drift, seemingly unaided, back to Naxos by way of Mykonos.

That deep Aegean Sea beckoned to her, a safe haven from the morbid marble statuary of Delos.

It was with a feeling of immense relief that they finally reached the sanctuary area, despite its history of despoiled graves and disinterred corpses. Those last few minutes, she thought she might pass out. Mount Cynthus had been beaten on one of the hottest days of the season. She could see that Steve was also visibly wilting. His camera had for some time hung unused from its neck strap, swinging to and fro as he negotiated the tumbled terrain. The panorama below them was magnificent, but Elizabeth was in no mood to appreciate it. She headed numbly for the sanctuary.

She had expected something more imposing, but it was merely more tumbled masonry. There was, however, a cave, albeit a man-made one. It consisted of a natural fissure with a pitched roof of large, dressed granite slabs forming a peak about six feet high. At the entrance there were also a number of smaller stones forming a wall and leaving a narrow passage into its twelve-foot depth. The most immediate thing Elizabeth noticed was that it offered the one thing that the whole of the rest of Delos did not: shade. She gratefully scrambled inside.

"I wonder if we'll have time to look round the museum?" Steve slid in beside her.

Elizabeth looked at her watch, frowning at the thought of a hasty scramble back down the hillside. "I don't think there's time..." She began to feel terribly tired and wanted most of all to sleep, just forty winks before venturing out. "I must have a breather, Steve." Her worried frown caught his wandering attention.

"Sorry, Liz, I wasn't thinking. We've still got an hour. You relax here for twenty minutes." He stood up. "I'll do a bit more exploring – around the old bone yard! Here..." He opened his rucksack and took out a couple of cans of beer, still reasonably cool despite the temperature to which they had been subjected.

"Oh, manna!"

"Forgot I'd brought them until now. Delos is a pretty striking place!"

Steve gave her one of his idiotic waves from his brow, like a drunken salute, with his head leaning to one side and a half-sick smile on his face. Elizabeth smiled at him encouragingly. He departed the cave, his body engulfing the light for a moment and making the interior suddenly very dark.

Elizabeth relaxed, savouring the coolness of the cave. She took the rucksack and bundled it behind her head, stretching out. Gritty dust clung to the film of perspiration on the back of her legs, but she forgot any discomfort as sleep insisted her eyes close and her mind begin to drift right-brain-wards, slowly spiraling into slumber, like a journey back through time's indefinable continuum. She snapped back alert briefly, her left brain rightly reminding her that she had not quenched her undoubted thirst with one, or possibly both, the cans of beer. The moment passed unfulfilled, and sleep mercifully came.

~

"Oh Jesus! Shit!"

"Mmnn..?" Elizabeth was, for some reason, quickly pulling off her shorts. Bits of sharp stone cut into her buttocks. A figure leaned over her in darkness, its face totally obscured. She could feel heat coming from its body and she knew it was a golden, beautiful body, like a classical Greek statue with its penis raised boldly, a small streak of semen glistening along its hardened underside. Her hand felt between her legs and came away damp. She gasped as the masculine shape moved forwards.

"Wake up!" She felt her shoulder being shaken vigorously, but not the expected penetration.

"Oh... Oh! Steve...?" She was at last awake and didn't much like the timing. "What's the matter with you?" It was only then that she noticed that in reality it was nearly as dark as in the dream. "What time—"

"We've missed it, damn!" he cursed. Elizabeth stood and ran to the cave's entrance. Dusk was beginning to carpet the distant sea a rich, wine-dark red from the setting sun. So, they'd missed their boat back to civilisation.

"Where've you been, Steve?" Elizabeth felt slightly angry, but it was tempered with a desire to laugh at the absurdity of their situation.

He looked her sheepishly. "I fell asleep as well." No more explanation was necessary. Delos had secured their undivided attention for at least the next eighteen hours.

"Perhaps they're still waiting," Elizabeth said as the realisation sunk in, but no, she could still just about discern the harbour and it was deserted. Nearby the museum building was in darkness. They were the only people left on Delos.

"I'm sorry, Liz." He looked like he genuinely was too. "We can sleep in this cave and be down at the harbour by midday tomorrow. We'll be back on Naxos in time for dinner."

Elizabeth examined her surroundings, but the dream she'd half remembered had decided her. "I'd rather not," she answered him. "Can't we find a place nearer the shore?" But of course, to trek down the hill in near darkness was foolish; it was bad enough trying to avoid the ankle-twisting, overgrown chunks of Delos' former glory in daylight. Before he could answer, she said, jokingly, "No. I know this is the safest place to stay now. At least we have shelter should it rain!"

They both sat quietly for an hour, saying very little. The sun finally gave up the day and the night was blacker than they could ever have imagined, except that there were stars in the sky, and over on Rhenea a few lights twinkled. A far cry, Elizabeth recalled, from Athens' bejewelled night, where every precious gem's colour was represented by streetlamps, houses, automobiles, displays, and sudden diamond-sparks from trolleybus cables.

Dinner consisted of a can of beer each – how glad Elizabeth was that sleep had saved them! – and a few biscuits and pistachios Steve found in his rucksack. They both ate and drank slowly; there was a long night ahead and it was still quite early. There'd be no browsing down by the quayside to find a suitable taverna. No embarrassed look around the owner's kitchen to choose their meal. No lingering, warm wash of wine and calm sea to lull the senses.

Later, the quietness began to make Elizabeth's flesh crawl. The atmosphere didn't appear to affect Steve, who was leaning, like herself, at the entrance to the grotto, breathing deeply and gazing enigmatically at the starry heavens. For some reason the expected rasp of the cicadas was absent and the sea was so calm and distant that any sounds it issued did not reach them. She felt far from sleep now yet yearned for a dream as powerful as that she had had earlier, as powerful as all her dreams had been whilst on vacation. She hoped that the cool night would not drive her inside the cave. There might be snakes in there now. She was reminded of the serpentine forms that writhed beautifully, yet balefully she thought, in mosaics on the floor of one of the roofless temples they'd visited; of scorpions and the whole spectrum of beasts which modern Western minds thought held evil intent, but which soared to god-like heights in the ancients' collective mind.

When she looked up again out of her reverie, Steve was no longer there.

Now where had he gone?

"Steve," she called gently towards the cave. There was no answer. The answer, she smiled, was simple: a call of nature. A small breeze cracked the dry grass at her feet and whispered around the sanctuary like a primeval, probing oread, wandering up the hill from its pleasures among the ruins and wondering at the strange being sitting in front of the atrium where once Apollo had been worshipped. Maybe that mountain nymph had seen no humankind for hundreds of years on those desolate Delos nights?

~

A mist was drifting up the hill and before he knew it, Steve was engulfed in its clammy caress. If anyone had asked why he had wandered off just then, he doubted he could consciously say. It felt the right thing to do, but the grey swathes curling around him were nightmarishly unreal on this warm night. He ought to return to Liz and try to settle down and get some sleep. Nothing could be done until morning. If he turned carefully, he could easily grope his way back without getting lost.

He took cautious steps, fretfully searching the ground for pitfalls, and in his concentration the lone, quiet yowl of a dog went unheard. Had he heard the sound, his myth-imbued mind would immediately have realised its portent. It was made only once, though, before the hag came to him. Hecate, the Goddess that Appears on the Way, was monstrously garbed in the apparel of a cadaver. Her dark hair like strings of snakes, her face dry and mummified, her eyes luminous shards. Under a shroud of fine-spun silk her withered breasts were clearly visible. His eyes met hers through the fog and he knew that time and reality had finally become spent forces for him. If the ritual purifications of Delos had been started by the Priests, these things were now continued under the guidance of Gods.

Delos was still a place where no living being lingered after dark and if the dead returned, it was to ensure that sanctity was forever preserved.

Steve was surprised at his mind's ability to think rationally as the corpse approached. Large hands, talons of aged flesh, reached to grasp his skull and he managed to scream only briefly as the cold, hard white thumbs forced their way between his lips and pressed his vibrating tongue down the back of his throat.

~

As the breeze died away a noise below startled Elizabeth, somewhere on the darkened slope of Cynthus. It sounded like tumbling stones or loose footfalls among the debris. Why would Steve go that far for a pee?

The night held a beauty that transcended her mundane thoughts. It was dark and alien, thousands of years old and still breathing a life as real as the lambent lights that now played over the remains of the cemetery. Elizabeth peered through the gloom, puzzling at the sudden flickering, flame-like flashes of light. Fireflies, maybe.

A glow seemed to lift above Hecate's Isle, or it may have been over Rhenea beyond. Immediately Elizabeth thought about the purification pit where Delos' long dead were relain. Loose chippings of stone began again to tumble down the slope, with the loud clarity only former silence can imbue.

"Steve?" Elizabeth stood and glanced around, finding only fear in her inability to penetrate the darkness. It was almost as if he'd never been here, a form as hallucinatory to her now as the city of Athens was. She began to feel anger at her descent into irrationality, but that descent was inexorable, driven by a growing terror at the dreamlike predicament she was in. She wanted to shout, to scream out Steve's name; he must be nearby. He must... Had he caught the boat back to Naxos and left her stranded with a mischievous facsimile of himself for a companion? It dawned on Elizabeth that Steve may never have been real...

Now she was being absurd!

She finally overcame her fear of the benighted hill and took to the friendless maw of the cave. She felt her way in, choking on the dust her shoes raised. Something – only for a second did her mind feel relief that Steve had returned – with strong, cold hands grabbed her arms and she could smell an obnoxious, a poisonous foetor from the darkness a little above her face. "Ste—!" But it wasn't, couldn't have been him.

The invisible figure was merciless in its actions, which Elizabeth quickly realised were those of something not living. Above all, the stench of death was forced into her nostrils and dry, crumbling flesh pressed down upon her. She was saved by the darkness from seeing the face that belonged to the hard, cold, half-slimy tongue which opened her lips and forced its attentions upon her own. Elizabeth felt silken fabric between her and the pressure of iron-hard breasts, and the posturing proboscis opening her jaws to cracking point while long-dead saliva dribbled down her throat. The sensation sent her reeling into the safe haven of unconsciousness, but not before her mind induced her to believe that this visitant to Delos was one of Rhenea's long dead guardians.

~

Dawn was like a red curse over the slopes of Delos. Steve and Elizabeth mused over it as they gazed hypnotically across the bay. They didn't really appreciate their changed viewpoint or their new flesh, such as it was. The vista from Rhenea was very familiar and had been for millennia. They sighed together, and gathering up age-tattered robes, made their way back down a long underground tunnel to join their purified brethren as the sun's strong light began to bask the empty slopes of distant Cynthus. They knew that Apollo's birthplace could never harbour the dead, or the living, for long...

Dead Water

Salin d'Aigues-Mortes, Petite Camargue, France

Brian stared at the gloriously vivid sunset across the salt marsh. Nature, he imagined, was in harmony with his emotions. In his fifty-two years he couldn't remember a holiday that had been more tranquil than this was turning out to be. Dreamy contemplations of environmental equilibrium basked him in a warm glow and filled him with contentment. And the holiday was not over yet – only half-way through in fact. For a while, he wasn't tormented about pollution, biological diversity out of joint, or his carbon footprint. The haze-rippled sun was low in the sky and red light flickered through the gently swaying reeds, stands of black spears silhouetted against the waning day. Through a gap in the reed bed the still water of the lagoon perfectly reflected the sky – crimson shading to pale azure blue above pink-tinted smears of cloud. The surface of the lagoon was so motionless, Brian saw, that sky and water might be interchangeable and if he stared at the mirror images for long enough he might never be able to tell the difference and the world would be topsy-turvy and changed to omnipresent exquisiteness forever.

The holiday in France was a first. For years, foreign holidays had been packaged and parcelled for two weeks in the summer, separating the working year. Managing personnel statistics for consumption higher up the chain of management was an endless round of achieving month-end deadlines and he was ready for a change, both personally and at the 'coal-face'. The latter was harder to achieve now that the years made him less eligible for promotion. But he was happy, nonetheless, and the holiday was a refreshing change from the all-inclusive, structured trips he was used to.

He and Harry had gone off for odd days or a weekend of bird watching, but this was the only time he and Jane had taken a two-week holiday abroad with Harry and his wife Brenda. When the idea had been mooted, Brian had been keen but wary, knowing from the experiences of other acquaintances how a friendship might be wrecked by the close proximity of those who had, a mere few days earlier, been the best of friends. Harry had taken early retirement, and his holidays seemed to take place with alarming frequency now he had more time on his hands, and *he* could afford, therefore, to have the odd unpleasant jaunt. And although he and Jane were very happy in their marriage, Harry and Brenda were having problems with theirs, which added to Brian's initial hesitation. Jane talked him around, however, and dispelled his qualms. Bless her. The two couples shared a car to the south of France and were staying in a chalet on a campsite in L'Espiguette, which, despite its relative luxury, still meant they were getting under one-another's feet for a couple of weeks. But neither disagreements nor arguments had arisen.

And the sunset was blessing that triumph, Brian thought. Jane was a gem.

Harry was starting to pack up, folding his piece of canvas, capping the lenses and putting his binoculars in their case. Brian would have liked to stay, basking in meditation in those final minutes before darkness decisively descended. He'd had a lovely day, but if they were to avoid ending up wading home through the marsh in the pitch black, they *should* really get a move on.

At least he might savour the day's salient moments while he packed up his kit...

~

That afternoon had begun sensibly enough, and it wasn't until they had ridden out past one of the reserve's bird hides and left it far behind that Brian's head began to feel the wrong shape. The sensation, he supposed, had either something to do with the landscape and the powdery smell of salt permeating the atmosphere, or there had been something wrong with the *moules marinière* he'd eaten last night at the restaurant. There had also been the curiously beckoning hand at the bird hide, which initially disconcerted him. Out of the dim interior, through the viewing flap, a solitary hand had gestured. Harry had dismissively declined the hand's invitation as they freewheeled on along the causeway, but then it presented its palm and splayed fingers, and shook wildly, as if waving goodbye. Or urgently summoning them back. The hand may even have been gesticulating at the warning signpost they cycled past.

Later, as he peered through his field scope, he began to feel decidedly odd; that sort of muzzy sensation that precedes a bout of vomiting and diarrhoea. He mustn't permit himself to become ill, he told himself, there was too much at stake.

He couldn't allow Harry to win the day, if indeed it was to be won at all. Harry always took a malevolent delight in getting the upper hand at bird spotting, as well as most other things in life.

Brian attempted to shrug off his growing queasiness and concentrate on the distant circle of landscape within the orbit of the scope's eyepiece. Although in sharp focus, the field of view appeared to be blurred. The scenery had an indistinct texture to it, as if it wavered slightly out of focus from other, more expressive patches of countryside. Something to do with the scarcity of trees, the lack of hills and the serene lagoons. The shimmering sheet of water bombarded the sun's rays back off its surface like an enhanced mirror, turning to an almost unbearably bright silver. Tall brownish-yellow reeds stood like a cluttered, thin army in disorderly ranks, motionless before the battle day to come.

"I wonder if the ladies are enjoying their ride?" Harry spoke quietly, edgily, without taking his eye away from his scope. His tripod was firmly positioned, and he was sitting comfortably in his fold-up canvas chair. Somehow, he'd managed to collar the best pitch on the small scrap of rough terrain. Brian's tripod stood on less firm ground, and his own seat squelched into the soggy surface whenever he shifted to make himself more comfortable. Yet they'd both agreed that the territory beyond the bird hide might yield better results, despite the deteriorating state of the paths and the warning notice they'd chosen to ignore. It was the instinct of the seasoned naturalist which led them to find the optimum locations, rather than previous experience of this particular part of the world.

Brian answered his companion's question with a grunt of acknowledgement, but he didn't say anything. Both their wives had opted for a horse ride, one of their must-dos on a holiday in the Camargue. He could see them in his mind's eye now, on their white horses, riding through grassy tussocks and along the beach, through gently foaming surf. Not his cup of tea, or Harry's. But that suited both couples. The wives could do their tourist things and he and Harry could get on with their preoccupation as twitchers.

And the *competition*.

Harry was one bird ahead. Brian needed to catch up with a sighting, and it must be a positive identification. It mustn't be any old bird. The Camargue was awash with, say, flamingos. They were a beautiful sight – white and pink, elegant walkers among the gleaming waters of the *étangs*. No, no, no. Brian needed a spectacled warbler. Or a collared pratincole. They would be worth twenty other species, even if there might be a bit of an argument between them as to whether a particular bird was in fact rare enough to qualify for the contest.

The friendly rivalry had been going on for years.

"Jane hasn't been on a horse for donkey's, has she?" Harry piped up again, seeming not to have noticed his inadvertent witticism. Brian wondered if his friend was trying to sabotage his concentration. He *had* been concerned about the rather casual way the riding stables had allocated the horses. And the two women found they needed specifically to ask for hard hats; they weren't handed out as standard practice. This was France, though, and their way of doing things were different to those in Blighty. The other riders, German and French mainly, had seemed rather surprised by the request, and to a man none of them called for protective headgear. Some of the younger riders wore their own cycle helmets, so Brian supposed their parents had foreseen some potential danger in riding unfamiliar horses.

"She'll be all right," Brian whispered grudgingly. He'd have preferred complete silence, both for the bird watching and his woozy head. Mind you, he allowed that the distraction might take his mind off the nausea. "They both will," he continued, and then paused, squinting through his eyepiece. "Your Brenda's not been riding for years either. None of us are teenagers anymore." Harry was Brian's senior by four years, yet was more haggard than his age would have suggested. Although nothing had been said or discussed, except between him and Jane, Brian believed that Harry and Brenda were no longer happily married, which might account for his occasional gloomy moods. Or perhaps it was simply that their marriage had reached that affectionless plateau that comes with years of living together. If Harry was anxious, Brian deemed it more to do with maintaining the marriage and stability for their two adult sons – who still lived at home – and hoping Brenda didn't have a riding accident, because that would upset their domestic arrangements.

Brian made sure not to lift his head from the eyepiece of the scope while they spoke. Perhaps Harry really was a little apprehensive about Brenda riding her first horse in twenty years, but was reluctant to admit it. Displaying anxiety wouldn't be his style. Either way, both men were here now and should be concentrating on the job in hand.

After dropping their wives at the riding stables, seeing them off with a wave and a few photographs as mementos, they had parked the car for the day and hired two pushbikes in Aigues-Mortes. With panniers loaded up with their equipment they cycled out into the wetlands of the Camargue. It was mid-September and the weather was still incredibly hot, which usually suited Brian. Except that now the heat was exacerbating his light-headedness.

He stared intently through his scope at the distant reed bed across a stretch of open water. Something, a bird hopefully, had been trembling the upright stalks and the thick clumps of grasses and might reveal itself in a moment. Unconsciously he scratched at a mosquito bite on his ankle, one of several that he had acquired last night at the campsite. He had forgotten to use the Jungle Formula insect repellent and was suffering the inevitable consequences. He was sweltering even in tee shirt and shorts, and the cloying heat seemed to intensify the itching, inflamed skin around the bites.

After a while his right eye tired of gazing through the spotter scope's eyepiece and he sat back in his chair and used his binoculars instead, to obtain a wider field of view, in the hope of catching sight of anything that might be flitting across the water. Surprisingly, there were hardly any interesting birds about. Three egrets stood dotted on a mudbank, as if waiting for a hand-out of food. To the far left, in a wide expanse of water, a small conglomeration of flamingos with their heads below the surface were sweeping the shallows for crustaceans. Whatever they did they seemed to do in unison. Whilst agreeing that they were a beautiful sight, especially in the great numbers you often saw in the Camargue, Brian always thought their thin legs and sinuous, down-turned necks made them resemble a bizarre art installation.

Harry had opened a lunch box and was spreading some goat's cheese on a chunk of baguette. Brian decided to wait a little bit longer before he ate, just in case his light-headedness *was* a precursor to the collywobbles.

The reeds managed to tremble in the afternoon heat, whispering and clicking. Old ghosts, Brian thought, their voices as reedy as the rushes themselves. Lean, skeletal wraiths, leaning together and murmuring about the two new visitors in their midst.

In the far distance, wading through the salt marsh, he watched a group of horse riders pass by, rippled by the heat haze. Training his spotter scope on them he confirmed that this was not the party in the company of Jane and Brenda.

Nine white horses and their riders trotted across his field of view, water spraying the flanks of the horses. Abruptly he realised that his attention had been diverted, and leaving the scope to idle on its tripod, he returned his binoculars to his eyes once more and scanned in slow, wide sweeps for fauna of the avian type.

They were in the west of the Camargue, not far from the *salin* d'Aigues-Mortes, situated in an area that combined salt lagoons, coastal salt meadows and small lakes. The topography was level and rather extraordinary. Colours were muted and defined by the yellow reeds, green grass, the pale blue sky and water, and the whitening effect of the salt. Most of all, Brian reflected, the relative seclusion made a person almost quiver with exhilaration at the wilderness. Tall reed beds served to hinder his inspection of far distances at low level in almost every direction, bringing on a sense of claustrophobia. The water was still and silent, except for the occasional muted sounds made by waders or muskrats swimming to and fro. There were three hundred and sixty square miles to this peculiar country, formed by the delta of the Rhône, the river itself creating a huge wetland island as it split into its petite and larger partner. The two spurs of the river meandered down to the Mediterranean, isolating the marsh from the disturbance of roads, traffic, and casual tourists.

Above distant rushes, Brian trapped a bird in his sights. It was gliding effortlessly and flew over the edge of the reeds and across the clear water in front of him. Then it dived with a sudden acceleration that was attained with breathtaking effortlessness, and he panned with the bird as it swooped low and nipped a dragonfly out of the air and then swept off back over the reeds and out of sight.

"*Hobby!*" Brian almost shouted. "Did you see it take that dragonfly? That's some kind of flying."

Harry failed to respond straight away, so Brian knew that he had seen the bird too, though not as quickly as him, and could confirm its identification.

"We're square methinks!" Brian said with a delicious satisfaction, taking a leaf out of Harry's book.

"Mmm. Not that uncommon though, Brian."

"Nor was your marsh harrier yesterday."

Harry had been lucky too, as they hadn't actively been bird watching then. They had been touring the *salin*, seeing the process of manufacturing the sea salt, when the raptor came sweeping across the pans of drying salt, the crystals tinted by the action of microscopic algae. The harrier's silver-grey wings and black wingtips starkly drawn against the surface colours of what had the appearance of diluted blood saturating the saline layers.

"Both birds are pretty much in the same league in this neck of the woods, wouldn't you say?" Brian's riposte was quick, before Harry could downgrade his sighting even more. "And the hobby is smaller and was harder to spot here, compared with where we were yesterday, I think you'll agree."

Brian slowly withdrew his notebook from his pocket and began to jot down the details, a description of the location, heading the entry with the bird's species and, taking out his GPS, noting the grid reference. He wrote slowly, waiting for Harry to reply, guessing the negotiations might take a while yet.

"All right. I'll let you have that one," his friend said surprisingly. Brian looked up to see Harry performing his theatrical knowing wink, creasing one cheek and curling his lip in the process. As if he was allowing a young novice the benefit of his doubt, in the full knowledge that both of them knew that Harry's magnanimity came out of sheer good will and not his agreement on the point in question. "It's *too* hot to argue one way or the other," he said heavily, scratching the long bushy sideburns that gave him the appearance of a country yokel, rather than a townie. "Shall we try another spot? I don't think we're going to see much more here." Harry paused. Brian sensed he was restless, but perhaps not on account of the rather paltry sightings. "We should be bagging a lot more birds!" he complained.

Brian smiled to himself, despite Harry's discomfort. Level-pegging! "Right-o," he replied cheerfully; raising his cap, he used it to wave across the water. "The path off to the left, if you can call it that, looks like it skirts round and closer to the other side of that clump of reeds. We might be able to add to our tally around there."

Suddenly he felt better. His light-headedness was gone. And he even didn't want to think about Harry and Brenda's relationship anymore. Harry regarded him as a bit of an old woman, with his fussiness and caution, but he wasn't going to mither any more about the misfortunes of others. Jane was right: he shouldn't fret about how others were feeling, deferring his own emotional needs to the greater cause of group harmony. No wonder his still abundant hair was turning grey. He couldn't hope to be able to penetrate Harry's thick skin, even if he might have been in a position to offer domestic guidance. His own relationship with Jane was a happy one, full stop. That's what life was all about.

So as not to make too much noise they loaded their pushbikes as quietly as they could and pushed them along the boggy path that circled the *étang*, eventually finding themselves in an area of much softer ground, with islands of reed breaking up brackish pools of water. The location appeared to be a very suitable one if they could situate themselves in the wedge of reeds without either disturbing the fauna or sinking into a quagmire.

Both men left their bikes on the raised bank and sloshed quietly though shallow water that smelled of decay and brine. They took just their binoculars with them this time and a piece of tarp to sit on, taking up position in the little stand of short reeds surrounding a tamarisk tree, whose drooping, grey-green wispy leaves would break up their outlines, yet allow them to scrutinise the nearby beds. They had been so careful that even a heron idling nearby had not thought to be disturbed by their approach.

The downside to the location was the number of flies, which appeared to prefer where they were sitting rather than discovering the abundant horse manure along the distant causeways. At least they were not the Camargue's notorious mosquitoes at this time of the day, although Brian wasn't sure whether the mossies hereabouts kept regular hours. The flies could be put up with, though their buzzing twanged a train of thought that threatened to take his mind completely off bird watching.

Earlier in the week, when the four of them had been touring the ancient fortress town of Aigues-Mortes, Brian had learned about the "tower of the salted Bourguignons" and a horrific episode during the Hundred Years' War. Planting the bodies of the defeated Burgundians in the shallow, foetid swamp in the thirteenth century was not an option if the rest of the population wanted to remain in good health, so the Armagnacs stuffed the corpses in the tower and preserved them with layers of salt. But Brian never found out what happened to them afterwards. It was never explained, but at some point those bodies would have had to be removed from the tower and be disposed of. What if they *were* secretly deposited in the salt marsh? To be feasted upon by fish and birds and muskrats and flies... Getting rid of your enemies in the marshes seemed somehow the more sensible option to Brian. He could imagine that, down the centuries, enemies, robbers, vagabonds, murdered waifs and the politically assassinated might become the disappeared of their time. Rotting, stinking, maggot-bloated corpses, floating to release the multitude of flies, then sinking and decomposing, eventually providing nutrients for the swamp's flora. And so, with that grisly image, Brian's day wound leisurely towards its end...

Thankfully, the magnificent sunset had diverted his thoughts...

By the time both men had packed up their

belongings and it was very nearly dark, they discovered – and sod's law determined it be so, as Harry tut-tutted – that their hired pushbikes came without headlamps. Ordinarily, if they had been at home, Brian would have carried the torch he always kept in his rucksack along with a first aid kit and penknife.

The threads of cloud that had made the sunset so fantastic had metamorphosed into a grey duvet. The light was fading fast as the Earth turned its back on the sun.

"We'll have to walk the bikes back out." Harry said wisely, if rather tetchily, realising that it would be foolhardy to try to ride the narrow uneven causeways between the swampy ground and the salt pools.

"I think I can retrace the path we took just to this spot," Brian said uncertainly, "but I'm damned if I can remember all the other twists and turns we've made today." He then recalled the location of the bird hide, and the warning notice they'd passed near to it. A worn, hand painted wooden sign, a crude red circle with diagonal and with faded words below: *danger – passage interdit.* There had been some sort of illustration within the red circle, but it was so worn away it was impossible to say what it represented. It might have been a depiction of a mosquito. That would have made sense, Brian reflected.

"If we can get back to that hide," Harry said, also remembering its position, "the paths should be pretty straightforward." The nervous pitch of his voice didn't convince Brian. "Besides, from there we'll be able to see the lights of the salt factory," he added with more confidence.

If the salt factory was working at night and *if* the buildings had external lighting, Brian thought.

"I've got my mobile, if we need to phone..." Brian remembered, thinking aloud. Jane would be concerned if they were late arriving. They had set off without further thought and Brian was already sloshing in the brackish water as he attempted to keep his bicycle on the narrow track.

Harry was striding carelessly ahead, disappearing in the darkness, making Brian hurry. In a moment of distraction, he slipped and went down on one knee, but still somehow clinging onto the handlebars of his bike. The moon made a brief appearance through the clouds, reflecting off the spokes of the bike's raised front wheel. As it rotated slowly above him, flickering across the face of moonlight, Brian could almost believe he was watching an old black and white silent film. In the illuminated space between the spokes and the moonlight, black speckles were cascading between the reeds. Almost like drifting seeds, Brian surmised, but more aerodynamic, as if seeds could launch themselves in unison and move in formation, like starlings. Despite assuming this was a perfectly natural phenomenon in these lagoons, he instinctively ducked to avoid the flying formation.

Something landed on his neck and involuntarily he brushed it away. Whatever it was, it fell off.

"Hang on, Harry!" Brian called. He slapped the back of his neck for good measure, recollecting last night's marauding mosquitoes. And as if on cue, the itching started again with a vengeance. And yes, he could expect their attentions soon, if they weren't circling him already.

A sound came back through the night as the moon's light disappeared once more behind the sky's blanket. A squeal of noise, blaring and then juddering as if someone was blowing inexpertly on a saxophone. It had to be Harry's bike wheels squealing, or something else, not Harry. Leaning forwards to right his bike, Brian felt the front tyre thud comfortingly on solid ground. As he stood up, he began to push the cycle forward, with more care this time.

"Is that you, Harry, making that god-awful racket?" Brian shouted out to the silence that filled the open space like a vacuum. For a moment he wondered which species of owl or other nocturnal wildlife might have been calling out in that saxophone voice, in the dark, if it wasn't Harry.

A few more metres of solid ground were gained before water was spraying against Brian's ankles, and in a moment he was knee deep in swamp water. Trying to balance, he lost his grip on the bicycle and it fell over and sank. He began to fish around with both hands, like a flamingo dipping for shrimp. But his feet were stuck in the mud and he toppled over backwards trying to extract one of them. Both his legs came up as he fell, his feet kicking free, but minus their sandals. There was no panic, but Brian was not a strong swimmer and he spluttered, thrashing, until he was able to stand up again in the shallow water. He decided that if he had to pay to replace the damned hire bike, that would be preferable to drowning in a couple of feet of water and leaving the bill unpaid. As for his expensive spotter scope in the bike's pannier – well the salt water might already have ruined that. Flailing about, somehow he managed to struggle through the almost impenetrable, crackling reeds that barred his way, as if they were the ultra thin skeletons of the long dead Burgundians, resisting his passage. Finally, he stood on the causeway, dripping wet and gasping.

"*Harry!* For Christ's sake, I've fallen in! *Wait will you!*" His voice resonated as if it shouted against an absence, as if Harry was no longer there to reply.

There was another odd sound from farther along the path. He scoured his memories for an identification, a bird call that sounded like someone on their deathbed loudly drawing in their last two breaths. *One,* pause. *Two.* Then silence. Brian wondered if Harry had fallen in the water as well, but the noise hadn't been anything like splashing.

His tee shirt and shorts clung to him as if they were a second, loose, wet skin, chilling him. Water was dripping from his sodden underpants, but a warmer oozing from the back of his neck and down his forehead was more worrying. He reached up with one hand and touched his brow. Warm, sticky liquid smeared his fingers.

He tasted it and the metallic flavour was confirmation.

He must have hit his head on something as he'd fallen into the water, though he didn't remember a jolt of pain. Yet come to think of it, there *was* a tingling sensation on his scalp. Combing his fingers through his hair, he yanked his hand away as if he'd received an electric shock. What it had encountered was many globular objects, firmly *stuck* to his scalp.

If they had been mosquitoes he could have slapped and slapped. But these...things on his head were...disgusting. Tentatively he felt his hair again. Like very small *eggs*. Warm, alive. A heartbeat inside each one, Brian was sure.

Brian was foremost an ornithologist, but he knew a bit about invertebrates. He'd half expected Jane, having gone horse riding, to perhaps unluckily succumb to the attentions of one of what he believed was now on his head and neck...

And what now appeared to be crawling up his bare legs.

Legions of them.

Ticks.

Gorging on his blood and fattening themselves. The ones he now touched gingerly on his midriff, below his sodden, rucked-up tee shirt, *were* bloated. They'd been there a while without him noticing. His groin itched painfully and several things squirmed, along with his testicles. These were *not* your everyday horse ticks, that was for sure.

Brian experimentally tried pulling one off his paunch with thumb and forefinger, but despite being quite hard, it eventually burst open, smearing his fingers with half-congealed gore. The mouthparts of the thing were still attached to his skin and where it had sucked, it hurt like hell, as if the animal had injected him with venom at the point of its death.

Blindly, he flicked another of the creatures off him and the skin surrounding where it had suckled contracted with pain. He tried removing a few more to see whether he could stand the cumulative soreness of their embedded, harpoon-like probes, while he ran barefoot along the causeway. Within seconds came an agonising immobility. Brian envisaged nerve poison being injected into him in small, cumulative doses with each of the creatures he disposed of.

Dropping to his knees, he began to examine his exposed skin more methodically... and found there was not that much of his flesh left uncovered. Perhaps if he could remove them one at a time... acclimatise himself to the excruciating throbbing... manage to walk to civilisation and a hospital...

Just then he thought about Harry. A light he hadn't noticed before was shafting through the reeds in front of him. Perhaps Harry was right, the salt factory security lights were on! His surge of hope was dispelled when he saw a bicycle lying on its side and beside it, stretched out on the path, a humped shape, highlighted by thin beams from the distant lights. And as he watched, in the pallid illumination, as if drifting from the reeds with the determination of a group mind, more bloated little speckles cascaded. He comprehended that this was unquestionably a dispersal of sorts, but *not* the nocturnal scattering of seeds.

The body on the causeway wasn't moving, but the black spider-like clusters that concealed it were constantly twitching. Whether Brian's strength was diminishing because he knew it was Harry beneath the parasites, or because his own blood was being methodically drained from him, he wasn't sure. Shivering, with shaking fingers he began to examine his skin with a good deal more attention now that he could also see. *Everywhere* he touched, *everywhere* he looked, there was no familiar pale skin. Instead, warm, pulsing black ticks, all distended bodies and squirming atrophied limbs, hanging to him tenaciously with their mouthparts.

Not just a few parasites. A *plague*.

Frenziedly, he dug into the wet pocket of his shorts and prayed as he scrolled through his flip-mobile's phone book. Jane's number came up and the screen's backlight began to flicker intermittently. He pressed dial and waited. Even at the speed of light, delay occurred as signals were routed and re-routed through a multitude of phone masts. He bit his lip and shuddered anxiously. The stubble on his neck itched uncomfortably and his beard tingled as if he had a rash. Jane's voice suddenly burst in Brian's ear and he screamed her down wordlessly in his fright. Then silence. He looked at the display and bellowed again. It was as black as the lagoon water. Violently thumbing buttons at random, the instrument unfailingly failed to come to life. The salt water had finally managed to seep into the innards and wreck it.

Jane would be dialling him frantically now, frustrated and scared when his phone did not respond. Not nearly so scared as him. His terror brought Brian near to tears. A yearning swept through him. Desperation to reach out and hug Jane, to tell her that everything was going to be all right. But it wasn't going to be all right. Brian closed his eyes but was unable to close his mind to how inhuman he must appear. A breeze rattled the reeds around him; bones of the dead clustering to watch the show. The gathered ghosts of the earth goddess nodding wisely while nature began its rebellion.

At last, when the torment intensified so much that Brian began to lose all sense of his surroundings, he rolled over and sat down. But even with the satisfaction of crushing many of the blood-sucking creatures beneath his buttocks, he knew – assuming he was still able to move his arms and legs – it would be pointless to try anything so dramatic and excruciatingly painful with rest of his body. Even less could he contemplate using his infested fingers on the vigorously gripped, unbearably pulsing skin of his face, lips and eyes.

Mount Ida, Iraklion region, Greece

The car shuddered as it climbed the road, up the southern flank of Mount Ida. Old potholes and recent rock-falls were a constant hazard but not nearly as unnerving, Damon thought, as the thousand-foot drop that he could glimpse at every turn. Nor, if he admitted it, were they as terrifying as Ron's driving.

Damon had thought it a bloody miracle that they had reached the middle weekend of the holiday without writing off the hired car, and even more miraculous that there had been no arguments: until yesterday. He looked out of the side window dully, dust adhering to the glass as if it were sweating as much as he. In the distance, the green vista of the Messara Plain was hazed by the blinding sunlight.

With Zaros behind them, Damon thought he could relax and forget about the row. He had hoped today's trip would herald a pleasant second week, with the argument forgotten, but now the details came flooding back.

Ron's driving was erratic, his swerving less to do with the omnipresent potholes than with his speed. Damon reached across the rear seat and took Susan's hand in his, hoping it would help him relax. They exchanged a smile before Susan returned her attention to the view. His wife was still angry at the things that had been said yesterday, he could tell, but she was doing her best not to let them spoil her day.

The road curved, looping back on itself and back again as it climbed higher. They'd had to keep the windows shut because of the dust, but now the air was clearer and Emily rolled down the front passenger window. Gusts of refreshing air blew in.

"Phew!" Emily removed her straw hat and held it out the window to dry off the sweat. Without turning, she shouted "What's this place? Where we're going?"

Before Damon could reply, Ron interrupted. "Wherever it is, it'll suit you two I s'pose. I just hope there'll be somewhere to get a drink."

"At least we're starting to catch up with Dam's itinerary," Susan responded sharply. She may have had some sympathy for Emily and her condition, but when it came to Ron, she knew the philistine for what he was.

Nevertheless, Damon screwed up inside. The argument could flare up again, at any moment, if he didn't defuse the tension. As he wound down his window, the smell of wild thyme filled the car. Rocky outcrops blazed in sunlight. In the distant valley the green fields appeared to glow with artificial light, as if the whole landscape were sharing two realities, splitting the two couples up again.

If he admitted it, the row had been partly his fault. Long before the holiday, he'd worked out an elaborate itinerary. The fortnight had included days of sunbathing and shopping, interspersed with visits to archaeological and historical sites. Yet somehow the cultural part had been all but sidelined. Emily had complained at Gortys that the ground was too steep and it was too hot to wander around a 'load of old ruins'. She had invoked her MS as the excuse; yet there had been days in Agios Nikolaos when she and Susan had traipsed for hours around the shops, while he and Ron sat in a shady little bar. And at Iraklion's street market; her multiple sclerosis had appeared to be still in remission then.

Damon had seethed as he'd watched the contents of his itinerary disappear with the days. Finally, he'd played his face. When an expected trip to Kato Zakros had evolved into a visit to a doomed banana plantation, he'd flared up, waving his neatly typed schedule at his friends as evidence of the exclusion of *his* bits.

The ensuing slanging match must have been heard halfway around Crete. With dying banana palms waving in the background, each couple had exclaimed the selfishness of the other, each screeching higher to drown out the other's expletives.

As the heat exhausted the quarrelling, Susan snatched the car keys from Damon – he'd been due to drive them back to town – and threw them at Ron. "Here, you take the fucking car, we'll find our own way back!"

That same evening at the apartment they'd patched things up. Damon had found it embarrassing, but bless her, Susan had taken the initiative. Afterwards the four of them had gone to the crappy taverna Emily liked and Susan had continued to act the diplomat over the grilled fish.

"I'm sure there'll be a bar somewhere up here," Damon said to the back of Ron's head. Actually, he wasn't so sure. The road was climbing steeper and rougher, glimpses of Mount Ida hazy in the heat and looking suspiciously uninhabited.

"You *still* haven't said where it is we're going!" Emily broke in petulantly.

"Vrontisi monastery." Saying that made Damon rack his brains about what it had said in the guidebook.

"At least it'll have a roof on. And four walls. And floors," Ron barked with laughter and Emily joined him. If this was a little joke at his expense, Damon felt he could rise to the bait quite easily. Susan squeezed his hand, sensing his thoughts.

"I suppose you have to use your imagination," she said unexpectedly, "when it comes to the palaces. Visualise how the buildings might have looked in their day." It didn't come out like a rebuke, but Damon felt secretly amused by her reply. What more *did* they expect to see of buildings three thousand years old?

"Fuck!"

The car swerved. The narrow road had swept up to an unbelievably steep incline, which then turned to the right at ninety degrees. Ron only just made it, and Damon had a few seconds of vertigo as he stared in horror at the vast open space below them.

"Fucking Greek fucking roads!" Ron was humping himself in his seat, elbows sticking out like inflamed daggers, as his large hands spun the steering wheel and the car's momentum slowed. Gravel spurted from the wheels and a cloud of dust disappeared behind them over the abyss.

"I need a fucking beer."

Damon's whole body glistened with the sweat of fear and anger. The last thing he thought Ron should have was a beer.

"It's part of the charm of the place. It'd be pointless coming here if it looked like England." Susan's statement was delivered seemingly without malice, but her hand trembled in his. "We just have to drive more carefully."

"Ron couldn't be a more careful driver!"

Emily scolded, flapping her straw hat. "He drives for the Social Services, remember."

All well and good, yet for the whole of the past week he'd tailgated other drivers and railed at their lack of courage. Damon willed Susan not to respond, but before she could the road wound past a roadside shrine and they were in the village of Voriza. Damon looked at the houses, their white-painted facades scummy with brown dirt. And sure enough, Ron found a bar: perched, it appeared, on the very edge of the Mountain. The four of them sat under a tattered sun umbrella in a walled-in garden, grateful to be in the shade. The garden's low wall gave a magnificent view south to the valley, and he wondered how he could do it justice with his camera while Ron ordered a round of drinks from an old Greek woman.

Shortly after ordering, a man arrived with the drinks, and with dishes of cool tomatoes and cucumber and a bowl of olives. Damon ploughed into the olives while the man unexpectedly drew up a chair, sat down, and produced a thick wad of dog-eared photographs.

Ron and Emily had snorted with derision as he began to pass them around. Susan, however, showed enough eagerness to encourage him. Not that he needed encouragement: the pictures had been touted to tourists many times and were obviously his pride and joy.

Although the sun had bleached many of the pictures, their constant theme was tediously obvious. All the photos were of couples or groups, sitting at this taverna.

"Dimitris." He pointed to himself posing in one of the photos. "You like to take picture?" he added.

"I'll do it," Damon said and swept his camera from the table. Dimitris dragged his chair next to Susan and ushered Ron and Emily closer together. After the film spooled a couple of frames, Damon wondered whether he would actually make the effort to post or take the photos back to the taverna. Many people obviously had done.

At the table, Dimitris' photos were becoming monotonous when Damon noticed a familiar face on one of them.

"That's, oh, whatsisname... from *The Holiday Programme*. Years ago." Damon stared at the creased, square white-framed photo, its colours faded out. "That's it. Frank 'I love Windscale'

Bough. They must have done a programme here."

"Uh?" Ron asked through his beer glass.

"Windscale, Seascale, Sellafield. They change the name every few years, hoping people will forget 1957. I seem to remember Frank Bough being very pro-nuclear power in the seventies. So, I always thought of him that way. He used to do *The Holiday Programme*."

"You said that," Emily piped up. Damon could tell she was struggling with the significance of the year, but didn't like to show her ignorance.

"Fuck him," Ron said.

It took Damon a second to realise Ron wasn't talking about him.

When Dimitris left, his snapshots exhausted, they sat in silence – and the quiet, Damon thought, was wonderful. No-one stirred in the village and the absence of traffic noise or radios was wonderfully calming.

"It's so peaceful here." Emily had noticed the atmosphere almost as soon as Damon. He saw that she was gazing at several clay planters perched on the wall, bright with blossoms. That could make the photo, he thought, standing to take a picture.

"How far now to Bronte monastery?" Ron asked.

The SLR's shutter clicked and the film wound on with a wheeze. "*Vrontisi.*" Damon clenched his teeth as he returned to the shade. "Not far. A few miles."

"I think we'll stay here a bit and have a rest," Emily chirped in.

"It is a wonderful spot." Susan stretched back in her seat and drew in a lungful of the breezy Mountain air. Damon began to relax too. After a second beer he thought it safe to mention the monastery, just in case either Emily or Ron suggested they'd gone far enough up Mount Ida and they should call it a day.

"The monastery dates from the fifteenth century, so it should be interesting." Damon hoped rather than spoke from sure knowledge. He tried to recall other facts in case he needed them.

"Didn't you say that some famous Greek painter had something to do with Vrontisi?" Susan asked, keeping the subject going.

"Yes, Mikhail Damaskinos painted six famous icons, but they were moved to Iraklion in the nineteenth century to escape the

Turkish invasion. The Turks destroyed everything else, including the library that was once there."

"There won't be much left to see, then." Damon ignored Emily. These oft-repeated words were becoming her mantra.

"At least there'll be walls and a roof. And floors!"

Tired of their sniping, Damon chose to ignore both of them. Bees buzzed near the blossoms, and their drone merged with the drone of the muted conversation between Susan and the others. He began to feel utterly relaxed, for the first time that day.

As he snoozes, Damon observes Zeus in the Diktean cave. Minos, one of his three sons, carving the tablets of the law while Damon secretly watches. When Minos sleeps, Damon throws the tablets into an underground well and chisels them anew with his own version of the laws.

The scraping of his chisel becomes the drone of bees and light invades his darkness.

"The sleeper awakes." As he opened his eyes, Ron shoved another glass of beer towards him.

"Dreaming?" Susan asked.

"He always is," Emily countered, as if imagination were a crime.

"For a moment I was with Zeus and Minos."

"Fuck miners, let's drink up and get to old greasy monastery."

"Vrontisi," Damon felt he had to correct, but under his breath.

~

There were no other tourists at Vrontisi and for that, Damon was grateful. Ron had a habit of displaying his ignorance in a raucous, condescending voice, one that made Damon cringe with embarrassment.

Ron had parked the car right next to the entrance, blocking a good photograph of the Venetian fountain.

Once through a gateway guarded by two massive plane trees, Vrontisi's simple bell tower rose before them in a courtyard of plain grey concrete.

"Is this it?" The tone of Emily's voice was at once derogatory and exasperated. As if Vrontisi's unsophisticated architecture symbolised the whole holiday. The holiday that Damon had urged they take.

Ron was about to add his tuppence worth when the monk – Vrontisi had only the one, Damon recalled from the guidebook – emerged from a more modern building to the left.

"Deutsche? English, yes. I will tell you about Vrontisi. Then I will show you Vrontisi monastery." The monk ushered them to a long table with benches, shaded by palm trees. He was about their age, Damon guessed, heavy, with a thick, dark beard wreathing his chin. He was wearing a black cap and a black tunic that skirted dusty calf-length boots.

"First coffee." Damon was pleased that the monk had managed to silence Emily and Ron for once. They sat sipping Greek coffee as the monk raised an index finger to gain the visitors' undivided attention.

"Today is an anniversary. So, I tell you a special story of Vrontisi. It is a story of *blood*."

Damon was intrigued. He could tell that Susan was, too. "In sixteen sisty-nine to eighteen ninety-seven, Crete ruled by Turks. By, how to say, Turkish Cretans." The monk smoothed coffee out of his bristling moustache with a thumb and forefinger and he pondered. "Turks who were Cretans."

Ron started to look glazed, uninterested.

"In that time, these Janissaries did not recognise Ottoman rule and there were many massacres."

"What are—"

The monk held up his hand to silence Emily. "The Janissaries – soldiers of the Ottoman Empire – recruited from Christians. The *Ambadiot* Janissaries lived by blood and terror. This is a story of Vrontisi and the Ambadiots, who lived in the villages around Mount Psiloritis." Mount Ida, as it's now known, Damon reminded himself. "In those days there were many monks at Vrontisi and when the Janissaries came on their horses, we were forced to feed and shelter them. If it was after their raiding, they would bring Christian girls to the monastery and..."

A cloud slid across the sun and the whole courtyard was coated in shadow. The monk rose from the bench and began walking up and down, scowling and wringing his hands.

"I tell you, we monks took so much and no more!"

A breeze rustled the fronds of the palm trees, as if trying to shake off the shade into which they had been plunged. Damon watched the wind ever so gently swing the two bells in the open bell tower. They might want to ring out, it seemed, but the monk's growing agitation gave them pause.

"The next time they came, the Ambadiots were alone. We fed their horses. We said to them to join our festival and offered much food and wine. The Janissaries ate a rich meal and drank our wine."

Ron clattered his cup into its saucer to indicate his growing boredom. If he deliberately wanted to break the spell the monk was weaving, he would fail, Damon thought.

"They drank wine and fell into deep sleep. In this courtyard, they were." He spread his arms to indicate. "We waited. We rose up from hiding, with axes and daggers. We – men of God – *butchered* the Janissaries in their sleep. *Their blood ran in rivers.*"

"God," Susan said. "I mean – how awful."

Damon glanced at her and smiled. He was enjoying the story, enjoying the way the monk spoke of the events as if he had been there to witness them.

Both Ron and Emily squirmed in their seats.

The monk might have interpreted their discomfort as a sign that his story had affected them too. Damon knew otherwise.

"The horses? We set them free in the Mountains. The mutilated corpses? The corpses we took to a cave now called the Tomb of Chalepa. And we threw them into the cave. We left Vrontisi. We took the icons and left the monastery, because there would be, how to say... reprisals."

Ron feigned a yawn. "Yeah. I saw the film."

Ron's facetiousness would be lost on the monk, Damon hoped. "What a fascinating story," he said.

"And a terrible one," Susan added.

"Can we see this here tomb?" Emily was hoping to catch sight of a few dead bodies to make up for missing her Saturday night horror videos.

"Today is the anniversary." The monk sat beside them again and the intensity of his gaze unnerved Damon. "It was justified, what was done." Then: "Today you will see the monastery *and* the cave. Which first?"

"The cave!" Ron and Emily chorused.

No contest then, Damon thought dismally.

"And then the monastery," Susan sliced in. Good for her.

"One kilometre to walk," the monk said as he stood and began the journey. Damon looked at the landscape, the slopes and rocky outcrops. Easy for Emily, since she wants to do it, he told himself waspishly. In fact, even Damon found the walk strenuous.

The heat bore down relentlessly as they plodded in a single line following the monk. The landscape was of cracked and jagged rocks interspersed with withered olive trees. Damon imagined it was a landscape blighted by its history.

The ground began to dip into a small valley and unceremoniously, the cave was before them.

"The tomb of the Janissaries," announced the monk.

Twenty feet below where they stood, bare, jagged horizontal slabs of rock bordered a fissure in the ground. At one time olive trees and scrub had hidden the hole from view, but now desiccated branches clambered only thinly over the exposed rock. The cave was not how Damon had assumed it would be. This appeared more like a small cleft than a cave.

"Can't we get inside?" Ron's growl sounded disappointed. Damon felt the same. It might be no more than a hole in the ground, but it looked like it might need mountaineering equipment to conquer.

"Is it deep?" Emily asked, no doubt thinking of her health and whether it was worth invoking it now they were here.

"I'm sure it'll be too difficult," Susan concurred. "There's still the monastery."

"No, no, no." The monk began to scramble down the slope, disturbing scree, which tumbled into the cave with a hollow rattle. "Here, you come, my friends? Yes." The monk was clearing away some pieces of twisted timber before Damon realised it was a makeshift ladder, which the monk began to slide into the cave. "We go inside!" From the knapsack he carried with him, he produced a handful of church candles and a disposable lighter. "Who first? I pass the candle."

Awkwardly, Ron was helping Emily down the rough ground, and Damon was amazed that she actually wanted to explore the cave. When Susan began her descent, he raised his eyes heavenward and thought, go with the flow.

"Coming, are we?" Ron bawled up at him, and

there was a faint echo as his words descended into the fissure.

Damon felt uneasy. There was no sight of the monastery from here. All he could see was the ravine through which they had passed, choked with gnarled trees and gorse. There was an emptiness and silence that in other circumstances Damon would have appreciated. Now the isolation, the distant mountain peaks and the cloying air of the ravine sent a shiver up his neck.

If they had an accident up here, no-one would come looking for them.

"Maybe one of us should stay above ground." Damon's words sounded insipid.

Below, Ron had already disappeared into the cave and Damon thought he could see the glimmer of a candle flame. A hand reached up to help Emily, who had begun to negotiate the ladder, her weight making it creak alarmingly.

"Many tourists come. The cave is safe." Damon wanted to believe the monk, but somehow he did not think that there were that many visitors, not with the walk here and the lack of facilities.

When Susan began to climb the ladder,

Damon quickly tried to forget his misgivings and scrambled down to the opening.

With candle in hand, Damon felt oddly like he was about to enter a hallowed place, the candle an offering to ancient gods. "You go. I follow." The monk's booming voice allowed for no dissent. "You wait at bottom. All wait," he shouted down.

When Damon reached the floor of the cave, wondering how Emily had managed the ladder, three disembodied heads greeted him. The flickering candles threw the background behind them into greater darkness. As the ladder rattled behind him, he suddenly feared that the monk was about to withdraw it and leave them stranded in the cave.

"Welcome to the cave of the Janissaries," the monk intoned. "You follow."

The monk's candle strode ahead, the skirt of his tunic flapping like a bat's wing in faint light.

The others trotted after him, their candles stumbling to keep up. Damon followed last, lighting up the floor, which was worn smooth as if by the march of many feet. As they descended, it grew wet with the constant drip of water from above. The vaulted ceiling was never far above and did not widen. The slick rock was white or occasionally rusty orange and was coated with stalactites imitating organ pipes. To either side, mounds of stalagmites stood like blighted grey fungi as Damon's candle flame threw them into relief.

The monk was silent as they made their way down the slippery incline. With every carefully placed step, Damon became uneasy. This tour was not turning out the way he had expected. Places of interest, even caves, felt safe. They had electric lighting. Handrails. Things like that.

Ahead of him, Susan had slowed her pace. She turned her head briefly, and Damon's candle revealed her creased brow and a nervous gleam in her eye. He put his hand on her shoulder as if to reassure her, but she jumped and nearly lost her footing, sliding three or four feet on the marble-smooth floor before regaining her balance.

"*Shit!*"

"Sorry..."

The sweat on Damon's face cooled as the temperature in the cave began to drop. They had religiously followed the monk, but for all he knew, there might be innumerable passages connected to this one. If the monk had a heart attack, would they be able to find their way out? None of the others was airing such questions and he contemplated doing so himself, even though Ron would undoubtedly find some wisecrack to flick back at him.

"I...I don't think...I can go..." Emily's voice faltered, coagulating in the slime from her lungs. She had turned around and was looking towards Ron, her round face mooned by the flame.

Damon had wondered when she would remember her illness. But now he didn't mind, because they could retreat without losing face.

"Oi! Mr. Monk. Wait a tick!" Ron's shout echoed around them.

The monk seemed oblivious and was a good way ahead of them, his flame dimming. Then he stopped and turned.

"My friends." He whispered. At first, Damon thought he was speaking to them, until he saw what the monk's light was illuminating.

"Blimey!"

"Look, Dam!" Susan said.

The monk had arrived at a semi-circular chamber, its walls wreathed in folds of stone like curtains. On the floor were the scattered bones of many human skeletons.

"The Janissaries?" Emily asked, forgetting she was exhausted for a moment.

Without thinking, the four of them had slithered down to where the monk stood. Damon had no doubt that these bones were the remains of the murdered Janissaries. The monk had been as good as his word. He relaxed a little, expecting the cleric to add further detail to his gruesome story.

But the monk was busy fixing his candle onto a natural shelf, using melted wax to hold it in place. On the shelf were three *kataifi* cakes – what Ron had insisted on calling, ad infinitum until it was no longer funny, 'shredded wheaties'. They looked fresh, and oddly, each had a small candle on top, like little birthday cakes.

Damon was half expecting Ron to regurgitate his quip when he realised what the cakes reminded him of: an offering. It was, he thought, as if the monk was making an offering. And this was, indeed, a sacred place.

By now the monk was lighting the cake candles and whispering a prayer that echoed around them. Perhaps the monastery had the tradition, because Vrontisi's monks had committed murder, of praying for the dead

Janissaries – and for the souls of the brethren. It made a kind of sense, though why hadn't the monk mentioned it?

The smell of burning wax began to fill the air, smoke wreathing about in streamers with nowhere to go. Skulls and limb bones surrounded them, bony fingers clawed against wet rock, as if struggling for purchase. Damon shrank from empty eye sockets, shadows shifting across racks of teeth. His gaze moved to where the bones lay in greatest abundance, piled up against the twisted hewn trunk of an olive tree.

"Dam?"

Damon was trying to figure what a piece of timber was doing down here and moved forward to get a better view.

"Dam. I think we ought to be getting back." The nervousness was apparent in Susan's voice, but Damon was not listening. His flame had revealed elaborate carvings in the tree trunk. Three female human faces, like masks, each pointing in a different direction. The style of the carvings was classical Cretan, far older than the Greek Orthodox, or for that matter the time of the Turkish occupation.

Damon felt a tug at the back of his tee-shirt.

"Damon. Let's get out." Susan pulled him farther away from the others, who had become mesmerised by the tableaux. At last, Damon was aware of Susan's terror, though it took him longer to realise his own. He was still wrestling with the meaning of the cakes and the carvings. What did they represent? Damon tried to remember his Greek myths.

Pulled again, he allowed Susan to steer him back up the cave. The monk was knelt in prayer before the little altar, the role of tour guide forgotten.

"What about Ron and Em?" he whispered in Susan's ear.

"I'm more worried about us," she replied. "Can't you feel it? This place?"

As one they turned and began to stumble as quietly as they could towards the cave's entrance. Damon's blood surged in his brain, adrenaline driving it now they were escaping, not merely returning. He turned once to look back, thinking that Ron and Emily deserved his help, even if he'd come to hate both of them. Then he saw *what* were escorting his former friends deeper into the cave.

"The little cakes are an offering, Damon."

Susan's grasp of mythology was much stronger than his. "They are known as Hecate's Suppers. She is often represented as a statue with three faces, or *three wooden masks on a pole*."

Behind them, Emily was screaming something unintelligible. Ron could be heard hooting, like a dog howling. Later Damon thought that it probably hadn't been either of them making those sounds.

"Hecate is associated with the underworld and with the ghosts of suicides and those who suffer untimely deaths." Susan hissed fiercely. "Let's not be included in her ritual."

Her words drifted across his mind as his gaze tried to penetrate the growing smoke haze below. Ron and Emily each had two escorts, grey and slender, strings of mummified muscle wrapped around bones. Bulbous heads perched atop pipe-thin necks, nodding to the rhythm of the monk's chanted prayer. Damon would always remember with a shudder the featureless backs of those grey skulls. Better that, though, than to have seen to whom his former friends were being taken.

Lake Como, Lombardy, Italy

They say there is only one island on Lake Como, but in fact there is a second. Isolo Melzi lies south of Como's crotch in the western leg of the lake and is accessible by a small ferry a half-hour journey from Bellagio. There are few sailings, the times and dates tucked away in the small print of the Lago di Como timetables. What inhabitants the isolo Melzi once had have long since departed; what is left of its architecture is of the type that draws few visitors. Indeed, the island rates no entries in Michelin or Berlitz and it is the fully sated holidaymaker who discovers it as a place to visit. The island's sparse details can be found in the slim leaflet available at the Villa Melzi, on the outskirts of Bellagio, to which it had an historical association.

"It says," Nigel said, "that there's the ruins of an Etruscan temple – might be worth a quick visit as we have nothing planned for today." Nigel was the sort that built his holiday around excursions. Trips here and visits there were derailed only by the call of vineyards and restaurants.

"You go if you like, Nigel, but I'm spending today by the pool covered in factor thirty." Tricia had already put on her swimming costume, wrapped herself in a sarong and picked up her towel bag. "We've done a million sights already; I need a day of rest." She poked him in the stomach through his polo shirt. "That needs a bit of sun, it's whiter than my bum."

Nigel grabbed her hand. "You'll get bored..." Tricia was a sun worshipper, so he really knew she wouldn't.

"Oh, I don't know. Some of the waiters here look pretty fit to me!"

He pulled her towards him and they kissed and fell onto the bed, Tricia rolling on top. "Is there something I can do to make you stay and rest?" She smiled and raised her eyebrows with mock innocence before kissing him.

Nigel surfaced and returned her smile with a

crooked one of his own. "You could tie me to the bedstead with your stockings and..."

"I could fuck you senseless so all you'd be good for is lazing around the swimming pool for the rest of the day... and probably the rest of the week!"

"Sold."

Nigel wondered why sex was somehow always better on holiday. Some psychological reason or trick of the mind, he imagined. Tricia lunged her hips up and down, the palms of her hands massaging his chest. He felt the surge coming in his cock as she pushed harder and faster and with a hissing outpouring of breath they both came. Tricia fell across his chest and stretched her hands up to his bound ones.

"I like hotels with brass bedsteads," Nigel said.

"When, exactly, did you become so depraved?" Tricia felt his penis begin to inflate again.

"Shall we have another go?" Nigel asked, ignoring her comment.

"I think the chambermaid's due any second. I could leave you for a few minutes while I see whether there are any sun beds left..." Tricia lifted herself off him, smirking.

"Well there's nothing here she won't have seen before," Nigel responded. "And I could ask her if she'd like to untie me, or perhaps..."

"...or perhaps she'll be the one with the wart, the moustache and the bosoms to suffocate with!"

"What a way to go!" Nigel couldn't help his arousal twitch at the thought. Perhaps he was a bit of a pervert? Aren't most men? He allowed himself the luxury of innocence when weighed against the wider masculine moral turpitude.

Tricia looked at him oddly, as if she'd measured his thoughts. She rose and began to slip into her swimming costume for the second time that morning. "I think you need a swim to cool off," she said. The high leg cut of her swimsuit enhanced Tricia's figure and as she bent to untie her stockings from Nigel's wrists, he kissed the beauty spot on her cleavage. "Or a cold shower."

By lunchtime Nigel was bored. He'd read thirty pages of James Ellroy, turned himself over several times to provide the sun with a fresh area of skin to bake, and swam frequently in the hotel's pool to cool off. Tricia lay resting on her elbows, her long hair cascading down her back.

She was reading a book through sunglasses that were so dark they would have been suitable for studying sunspots.

"Fancy lunch?" he asked.

"Not for me. I think I had too much at breakfast." He didn't respond for a minute and at last she turned to face him. "Food, not lust, you old lecher!"

"Less of the old, if you please."

"Why don't you get something to eat and I'll see you later," Tricia said, "but order me one of those cocktails before you go, there's a love."

Nigel caught the eye of a waiter and ordered her drink. "I think I'll nip to town and have lunch at the Piccolo Bar. The owner's a mine of information."

"And not too shy to share it with any tourist who happens to stray in there, willing or not," Tricia added trenchantly. Nigel liked the Piccolo, it was his genuine 'local colour'. "Well, don't let me stop you. I'm sure you'll be told the exact location of the most obscure villa in the region. The one with the most wretched paintings and feeble sculptures. That man's probably paid to recommend the least inspiring tourist traps imaginable."

Including the isola Melzi Nigel thought, but didn't say.

~

By the time he'd made the ten-minute walk to Bellagio, Nigel's thoughts had changed his mind about lunch. He skipped Piccolo's and went straight to the ferry terminal where he picked up a timetable. The last boat to isola Melzi was leaving in half an hour. He bought a *bigletto ritorno* and sat on a public bench watching the water, chopped by the modest little ferries as they crisscrossed the centre of the lake.

About a mile away, above the far shore, Nigel's attention was drawn to the tree-covered mountains that dominated the lake's hazy blue air. The sky was cloudless, shimmering in the heat. A black kite silently swooped nearby, hunting for unwary mallard chicks in the shallows. Behind him Nigel could hear the muted conversations of tourists at Piazza Mazzini's cafes, and the sound of a camera shutter working overtime. A young man stepped in front of Nigel. He was moving around, taking photographs of the departure of the *Lucia*. Nigel estimated him to be under twenty-five, ten years his junior and rather young for this type of resort. Bellagio was usually reserved for the well-heeled blue-rinses. The man's hair was short and blond in colour; his face liberally freckled. The battered straw panama on his head may have implied trendiness, but Nigel thought it shouted ostentation. Despite the hat's suggestion of youthful exuberance, when compared with the man's pasty complexion, Nigel's tanned skin and dark hair made him look the fitter of the two.

"Hello? You're at the Belvedere, aren't you?" the cameraman asked as he turned to face Nigel. The young man offered his hand, adding, "Alan. Alan Marshall."

Nigel shook the offered hand, standing to do so. "Nigel. Pleased to meet you." He vaguely remembered noticing the man in the hotel's dining room, eating his meal alone. There was a brief silence, in which Nigel thought he ought to add something. "Are you enjoying Bellagio?"

"Bit better than Leicester, wouldn't you say? You're from the Midlands too, aren't you?"

"Stratford." Nigel discerned boredom in the voice of his companion, as if he was unable to find inspiration for his photographs. "Are you a professional?" He pointed to the expensive looking camera hanging around Alan's neck.

"Attempting to be. I'm looking for a theme on this holiday that I can work up into a new portfolio." He waggled the camera as if it was a disobedient son unwilling to do its parents' bidding. Nigel noticed that Alan had a bulging gadget bag with him, no doubt containing more camera equipment. "You on holiday?" he asked.

"With Tricia, my partner. She's decided on a day's sunbathing," he felt he needed to add. Near the water's edge the kite caught his attention as it wheeled silently and then dropped towards the surface. It rose up again swiftly, something small and feathery in one claw. "Ah, you've missed getting a picture of that kite catching its lunch!"

Alan turned in time to see the bird soar off into the distance. "I'm not much on wildlife photography – more interested in architecture."

"Well there's plenty of that." Nigel responded. Then he added, without wondering why, "There's an Etruscan temple on isola Melzi – a bit off the beaten trail, if you're interested?"

"Where's that?" Alan asked, his curiosity aroused.

Nigel thought it might be good to have someone to talk to on the trip, even if Alan ended up being a bit shallow. "It's where I'm going now. The boat leaves in about fifteen minutes. There are only a couple of return trips each week, and none at weekends, as far as I can work out from the timetable."

"Yeah, *wow*. I think that'll be spanking. Mind if I join you? I'll just get a ticket!" Alan's enthusiasm was somewhat adolescent, but Nigel decided he could live with that.

Realising he ought to explain a bit more, in case Alan was expecting to see the Parthenon's elder brother Nigel said, "It's apparently a ruin. Might not be exactly photogenic."

As the *Lucia* – now well out into the lake – turned to the north towards its destination on the far side, so another boat hove into view from behind the Punta Spartivento, heading for the ferry terminal. As it manoeuvred, Nigel could see it was even tinier than the small car ferries that usually plied Como's waters. The *Monte San Primo*'s grand name certainly belied its nature. It was a foot-passenger ferry with no amenities other than a seating area and toilets. Almost as soon as he and Alan boarded, he began to have doubts about the sense of this trip. He had brought no food or anything to drink with him, and intuition reliably told him that there would be nothing by way of a pizzeria or trattoria on the island, let alone a mini-market, – even if there were, it would probably be closed for lunch.

Alan quickly made his way towards the prow of the boat and sat on one of the front-row plastic seats, plonking his camera bag down beside him. Nigel followed and sat next to the bag. Almost immediately he heard the chain being put across the gangplank to stop any further passengers embarking and a chill scurried along his skin, a goose-pimpling that was stirred by zephyrs from somewhere other than the erratic waters of the lake.

"A ruin can often make a good photo," Alan said, returning to Nigel's comment. "Atmosphere's what I need, and the right light." The boat's engine revved and it moved off, heading south. Alan raised his camera and began scanning the hotels along the shoreline.

"Well, perhaps you'll be in luck." Nigel glanced behind him and saw a scattering of passengers spreading themselves about between the seats. Mainly locals, by the looks, and mostly old men. There was a well-dressed Italian woman with a bright magenta headscarf that rippled in the breeze from the lake. And five other holidaymakers, two couples and a boy of about eight. They were all similarly dressed in tee shirts, shorts and baseball caps; it occurred to Nigel that they seemed an unlikely lot to want to see an Etruscan ruin on a very small island that had nothing else to recommend it. One of the men was extremely tall and was wearing ridiculously short shorts. How silly they looked, Nigel thought, but when he saw that the party were all toting shoulder bags of one sort or another it reminded him how unprepared he was.

He unconsciously felt in the pockets of his chinos. He'd got his wallet and some money, and his passport, but his hands felt unoccupied, as he hadn't a bag, a camera or anything else with him. He felt like he was going to work without his laptop or his briefcase. For a moment he panicked, as if he had found himself commuting home on the train and his computer had been stolen while he catnapped.

"Everything all right, Nigel?" his companion

asked. "You look a bit agitated." The lens of Alan's camera blinked at him and whirred.

As Nigel leaned forward to check his back pockets, he discovered the leaflet about the island. "No I'm fine, just thought I'd forgotten this," he lied, pulling out the document and unfolding it, before handing it over. He wondered how uneasy his expression would look when the developed snapshot revealed itself to Alan.

Alan took the leaflet and unfolded it. "'Isola Melzi. Temple of the Maenad. Now little more than a ruin,'" he read aloud. There were just a couple of paragraphs of text and no illustrations. "'The Etruscans were a short-lived civilization, occupying Etruria from the first century B.C.'" Alan stopped. "Never heard of 'em."

"Well I don't know too much myself, either. Other than what's printed there." The *Monte San Primo*'s engines began to gargle and she started to change course; with the adjustment the slipstream across the lake stiffened. Nigel's short-sleeved shirt felt completely inadequate and he shivered, even though the temperature must have been in the low thirties.

While his companion read on in silence,

Nigel stood up in the hope that moving elsewhere might lessen the curiously chilly wind. As he did so he became aware of the flapping of material, like a bright flag, and turning he was startled by the young woman with the headscarf, now sitting right behind his and Alan's row of seats.

"I couldn't help overhearing and hope you don't mind," she said. She spoke perfect English with her Italian accent. Nigel wondered briefly what it was he shouldn't mind.

For the first time he saw how beautiful she was. Her headscarf had at first suggested an older woman. She had amazing hazel and green eyes and her hair was a sort of dark golden brown. Her makeup was impeccable; her dress skimpy and short. In an instant he forgot the breeze.

"No, 'course not," Nigel almost stammered. The woman smiled in a friendly manner, but her eyes were mesmeric and somehow lacked the same emotion. "Do you know about the temple on the island?" he asked. She had obviously heard Alan reading from the leaflet. In any case, what else was there to see on isola Melzi?

"Why yes... a little," she replied. She leaned

forward as Nigel resumed his seat and his nostrils caught the aroma of her perfume. The smell was flowery and herb-like. "Of course, the Etruscan civilization did not really extend this far north in Italy. The temple there is the only example in the whole lakes region."

Nigel reasoned that she was a tour guide, on her day off. That would make sense. But why was she traveling alone to isola Melzi – perhaps scouting out the location for possible group tours in next season's itinerary?

"Hi." Alan had turned in his seat and was offering his hand to the young woman. "Alan. *Very* pleased to meet you." Nigel had forgotten his temporary buddy for a moment but was now perplexedly offended at his interruption.

The woman swiveled on her seat towards him, crossed her legs, but did not offer to shake hands. "Gabriella." Again, she smiled, and her eyes appeared to roam over Alan's features like an inquisitor. "You boys are photographers?" There was something in the way she used the word *boys* that, though it might have been an endearing affectation, came across as condescending. Alan did look boyish though, Nigel conceded.

"He's the photographer," Nigel blurted, trying to draw Gabriella's attention. Then he couldn't think of something interesting to say about himself without exposing a species of gormlessness. But he needn't have worried – Alan was waving his camera about stupidly, as if he didn't know what the thing was for and staring at the exposed flesh of Gabriella's thighs.

"Of course, there is not much left of the temple." She began to take up the conversation where she'd left off, glancing from one man to the other. "The Etruscans built them of terracotta, wood and mud-brick; fragile and perishable materials, you understand?"

Nigel nodded coyly, and as his gaze looked away, he noticed for the first time that several of the pensioners on the ferry were carrying wreaths and bunches of flowers. Was there a cemetery on the island, he wondered? It suddenly became very important to know for sure, and was a question he would like to ask Gabriella. For a start, they were all old men, no women, and all dressed in well-worn Sunday best.

"So, what was this *maenad*?" Alan found his

voice, pointing to the leaflet. "This hardly has any information."

"Hmm," Gabriella hesitated. "The temple name is perhaps a little misleading. Of course, there was a big influence from the Greeks on Etruscan culture. The temple is dedicated to Vegoia. She was one of the *haruspices* – soothsayers, you say – who read the entrails of animals."

If memory served, a maenad was some kind of woodland nymph, along with dryads and so on, but Nigel couldn't be certain they were of the same species. "So, she was what we would call a wood-nymph?" he asked, hoping to emphasize Alan's ignorance. He had to admit, however, that he wasn't even sure if the soothsayer Gabriella's spoke of was a character of myth or a real historical person.

"Vegoia was nymph-like, I suppose. The maenads were worshippers of Dionysus and so were sensual and artistic." Gabriella paused to remove her headscarf, which was threatening to take off across the lake. "She danced in pelts and – forgive to say – tore the raw flesh of wild animals to eat." Just then the wind dropped, and the ferry's engines rumbled into a different gear.

"Well, I'm sorry if I have bored you, but we are nearly there." She stood up and turned towards the aisle between the rows of seats.

Nigel stood too and, as the boat slowed and moved sideways in its own wash, he noticed the heavily wooded island close by. There was a small timber jetty, towards which the boat was attempting to manoeuvre. He returned his attention to Gabriella. "Can I just ask—"

"Yes?" she said, her eyes fixing his like superglue. There was still that frostiness in her demeanor, which made Nigel hesitate.

"The men, on the boat, with their bouquets. I take it that there's a cemetery here? Nobody actually lives on the island, do they?" There, he'd asked the question that had been perplexing him, but almost wished he hadn't, for Gabriella's expression became contemptuous.

"These idiots, they have their old ways. *Imbeciles*! Do not concern yourself. If they say anything to you, ignore them." She turned and quickly stepped off the boat, the side-split in her dress gaping provocatively. Walking briskly along the rough planks of the landing stage, she stopped and turned once to smile enigmatically. "'*Vestigia nulla retrorsum*'," she said.

Nigel thought her look was aimed at him, but Alan stepped forwards saying, "She can pose for me anytime!" He was grinning, his camera stuttering through multiple exposures. Gabriella was a stunner, but her beauty, Nigel thought, was only as thick as her skin. If Alan imagined for one minute that she'd ever consider posing for him, he was living in the land of the cloud cuckoo.

They were becoming huddled amidst the old men and the other tourists at the front of the boat, the slow-motion scrum for the landing stage halting their exodus. Nigel could smell the fragrance from the bouquets, combined with, of all things, the camphor smell of mothballs.

"Phew," Alan continued, "I'd rather be smelling Gabriella than this lot."

One of the old men screwed his head around as they all shuffled forwards. "She is not for you," he said in a heavily accented voice. "Why do you come here? Isola Melzi not for tourist."

And then they were on dry land and the *Monte San Primo*'s crew were already shoving the boat from the jetty, using the tall wooden poles which formed its verticals and which held the safety rope, which some of the older Italians were using to help them along.

Nigel looked ahead, but could no longer spot Gabriella. Whatever he believed, or what the information leaflet failed to say, there *had* to be some occupied dwellings on the island. Perhaps she owned a private villa?

"I'm not a tourist. I'm a *photographer*," Alan shouted back at the man who had spoken, but he either did not hear or ignored the remark. "What d'you think Nigel, as if the island belonged to *him!*"

"Forget it. We've got three hours and then we have to make it back here to catch the last ferry of the week." He gazed at the island. There was a narrow, dusty track that led up and disappeared into a grove of huge Atlas Cedars. Another small path led off to their left, hugging the shoreline, which became rocky and steep as it disappeared around the curve of the island. "Have you still got that leaflet, Alan?"

The locals were all heading in a procession along the coastal path, while the other holidaymakers seemed undecided what to do. Nigel could understand that. There was nothing here, no road signs, not even a poster suggesting a way to the temple. Not even a timetable at the dock giving details of the return sailings. He shivered, and anxiety welled up in him as if he had become a trapped animal. But the sensation was less well defined. A feeling of being ensnared that was more than just the sense of isolation that the island's unusual quietness suggested.

Alan returned the information sheet and he scanned its sparse content, desperate to find some reassurance in the printed words, reassurance that he knew was absent.

"What d'you think she said?" Alan asked.

"Said what?" Nigel looked up, distracted. "It says the temple is in a grove at the centre of the island, so I'd suggest we take the path straight ahead."

"You know, Gabriella. She spoke in Italian – about the codgers."

"Oh, that. No idea, but I think it was a quotation, in Latin. Sounded like it."

"She was something, though, eh?" Alan paused. "But chastity belt material. Tell you what though, if you want to spurt some spunk, there's a fantastic bit of skirt staying at our hotel. Gagging for it, she was."

Nigel often wondered why other men always felt the need to boast of their sexual conquests. At least if the sole topic of Alan's conversation consisted of innuendo and sexual exploits, he would only have to put up with it for a few hours. And it might take his mind off the vulnerability he felt, that threatened to spoil his visit.

When he didn't bolster his companion's ego with some apt comment, Alan continued. "I don't mind telling you, Nigel, it was the best sex I've had for years. Tied me to the bed, she did – with her nylons."

Nigel's stomach lurched. It was a coincidence. Had to be. Nevertheless, he had to ask, as casually as he could, "Oh... yeah and what was her name and room number?" He willed Alan not to say Tricia, putting on a calm face that masked a growing nausea.

Alan winked. "For me to know and you to find out." He laughed. "Actually, I never did get her name and we did it in my room. *Twice.*"

Nigel's head swam. This was nonsense. He could just ask Alan what she looked like, when the lovemaking took place, whether she had a mole on her left breast. It would prove things one way, or the other. But if...*if* it had been Tricia what could he do? Confront him with the revelation that his partner had fucked Alan? Engage in a fight with him, the outcome of which he couldn't be sure? *And* it takes two to tango. So, it would come down to whether or not he trusted Tricia.

Nigel's stomach continued to churn and he tried desperately to regain a sense of perspective. It was better not to ask, to hope that Alan's description was a coincidence. He wasn't normally the jealous type, he reminded himself. Despite this, he would remain wary of Alan for the rest of the holiday. He no longer trusted him, even without material proof.

"Do we know," Alan asked, "how big this island is? Have we got enough time?" He obviously hadn't noticed Nigel's discomfort, and was in any case staring towards the other tourists, who were following the Italians around the shoreline path. "Maybe they've got the right idea?" he pointed.

Nigel gave himself a minute to compose himself. "No, they have as much or as little information as we do. So, they're playing it safe and following the locals." Nigel hesitated, doubt invading his thoughts. "Let's see, it's two-thirty," he tapped his watch. "If we allow ourselves, say, seventy-five minutes. If we haven't found the temple by then, it'll be time to head back here for the ferry."

"And I'll use my notebook to keep track of any turns we make in the road," Alan added, extracting a pen and a creased notebook from his camera bag.

"Good thinking." The day was becoming a bit of an adventure, one that hopefully would allay his absurd misgivings about Alan. "Though I'd be surprised if this one-horse island has any turns in the road!" He managed to smile.

They set off and were soon surrounded by a screen of dense shrubbery and trees. Almost immediately the path began to climb and both men were starting to gasp in the cloying heat. Nigel peered around him, the close screen of greenery almost claustrophobic. The mixed woodland consisted of laurel, beech and oak trees, with various pines, blue cedars and myrtle shrubs – a landscape that differed utterly from the ornamental gardens of the villas around Lake Como. The woodland reeked of age, as if it was a piece of primal temperate forest left untouched by the Italian Renaissance landscapers.

"Hey, look at that!" Alan skipped forward to a heavily shaded clearing by the side of the path. He raised his camera to his eye and began adjusting the settings to account for the feeble light.

In the area of cleared ground was a stone statue, about five feet tall. It was of a woman, naked from the waist up, classical looking. She held a staff around which were carved wreaths of ivy. She was in a dancing posture. The statue was coated in lichen, pale green growths that resembled peeling dead skin. The stone eyes were blank, blind, and yet somehow scrutinized the surroundings as if they really were seeing. Its lips were voluptuous. Nigel shuddered. The thing was ugly, pagan looking, despite the swathe of stone garments that modestly hid the figure's inner thigh and legs. Some undisclosed meaning debased the classical form of the carving – the naked breasts, the long curly hair and the finely sculpted arms – an essence that escaped Nigel's consciousness, but that nevertheless pitted his deepest thoughts with blobs of anxiety.

Alan's camera shutter clicked away as he moved around to secure the best position for his shots. Once, the camera's built-in flash flared in the dim surroundings and the figure appeared to jump, making Nigel jolt in reality. This place was intensely creepy and he wanted to move on as quickly as possible. For a moment he even considered suggesting to his companion that they abandon the search and go back to the jetty. However, pride got the better of him and he pressed on, Alan following behind.

"Quite a piece, eh?"

"If you say so," Nigel replied.

"They're all over, too."

Nigel was about to ask what was all over when he noticed among the trees, dotted here and there, other stone figures mostly hidden in the dense foliage. He did not wish to hang about and was glad that it would be difficult to examine them more closely.

"They must be fakes," Alan stated.

Nigel thought about that. The female goddess, or whatever she was, had not looked phony. It appeared as old as time. "What makes you say that?"

"Well, think about it. This isn't exactly Disneyland. There's nobody on this island, aside from us and a few other tourists, yet if these were real Etruscan statues, we'd be paying through the nose to see 'em, or they'd be in a museum, not here."

Nigel thought he might have a point. Nonetheless the female figure with the staff had the appearance of age. "But why bother?" It was not really a question since as far as Nigel was concerned it answered itself. Why would someone bother to sculpt a load of statues and dot them around in woodland when it was apparent that hardly anyone, with the exception of the pensioners, ever visited the island.

As the path climbed yet higher into the heartland of the island, both men ceased talking and concentrated on catching their breath. The sticky heat made the air seem as if there was some noxious gas poisoning them. Nigel was becoming drowsy and needed to rest, but Alan was still forging ahead. Despite the temperature he did not want his dignity demolished by confessing to Alan that he needed to have a break, so he pressed on, agony building in the muscles above his knees. Although he was trying to deem today as a bit of a lark, he at last admitted to himself that it was a more serious adventure than that. Whatever dire tourist trap might have been recommended by the owner of Piccolo's Bar, it would at least have been safe and unthreatening. Unlike this island.

As sweat poured down his face and his shirt stuck to his skin like a layer of wet fat, Nigel started to feel ill. It was not simply fatigue. He'd had about three drinks with Tricia before lunchtime, but this was not the light-headedness of inebriation. He was woozy and his head felt enlarged with pounding blood. That could be because of the physical effort of climbing the steep pathway, trying to keep up with Alan. Stumbling on, his thoughts began to drain away with the perspiration that dripped from his face, and Nigel fancied he was drifting into a waking dream.

The trees appeared greener, their colours more saturated, but they were less in focus. If he had been drunk, he could have understood his strange feelings and the peculiar dense foliage. Instead, he just felt very odd, as though the foot-worn path was leading him heedlessly into danger.

Imperceptibly at first, the close silence was breached by a soft singing, a wordless series of long drawn out notes, like a flute, but decidedly human. For some reason Gabriella was brought to mind, the beautiful notes reminding Nigel of her beauty. The keening was both beguiling and disquieting. He sensed, in those moments, as the voice faded among the trees, that he more truly appreciated the atmosphere of the ancient wooded island. He had tried in the past to allow his mind to absorb the essential ambiance at many a monastery, church or villa, but had failed. Until now. Despite his queasiness, he intuitively understood the elemental atmosphere of the island. An ancient place of pagan ritual.

When he thought he glimpsed an animal in the woods, he at first assumed it was a hallucination. Nigel's eyes darted as the creature itself darted through the underbrush. In the fleeting glimpse he saw something bulky, very hairy and scary.

"Did you see that?" he called to Alan. His voice sounded thick, muffled. And as Alan did not reply, he imagined it was. As soon as his concentration turned towards the path again, he saw another animal among the trees, or perhaps the same one. Except this one was on the other side of the path. There was a rustling sound, followed by an almost inaudible grunting. Whatever it was it fled into denser undergrowth, leaves and branches clattering like broken glass.

Nigel broke into a run, as best he could. But it was as if he was loping through thick olive oil. His pace slowed almost immediately and he dropped to his knees, his chest heaving. He found he had reached the crest of the hill and the path before him began its descent. Nigel looked through the mist that glazed his eyes. In the woodland glade below was the temple of the maenad. Alan was already stepping into the ancient structure. Scattered along the front step and leaning on the jagged, ruined columns of the portico were the bouquets of flowers and the wreaths. The old men had already been here.

Nigel stood up and stumbled forward, stopping before he reached the truncated pillars of the portico. Carved around them were wreathes of ivy, motifs reminiscent of the statue in the woods. The temple itself was roofless, and beyond the porch there appeared to be a single room, of which only part of the rear wall remained. On this wall were fixed three larger than life heads, made from terracotta. There was a smirking male face with what looked like a fool's cap carved in the shape of a bull's horn, and another male, this one more menacing, with a full beard and an animal's ears. The third figure, in the centre, was of a woman's face, oriental looking, with large wide eyes, a long nose and sensuous mouth. Her head was fringed with long tresses and above them rose the scalloped fan of a headdress, carved to resemble shells or perhaps idealized leaves.

There was something about the faces that stopped Nigel advancing any nearer. He was afraid like he'd never been before. The leering faces were horrible, but he didn't know why they disgusted him so much. It was as if awful secrets were brimming within their antique lines; awful secrets that were so overwhelming that the faces could no longer contain them and they spilled into his thoughts. Even then he could not comprehend what they meant, as if he'd suffered a species of brain damage and could not collate the images and thoughts into any sort of coherent understanding.

Alan was passing across the temple, between the broken pillars and the wall of the faces, but jerkily. It was as if he was shivering with exposure. He looked once towards Nigel with a very peculiar expression of surprise, as the eerie singing began again. In the blink of Nigel's eye, he disappeared.

He no longer cared what Alan was up to. He wanted to leave. *Now.* Just get his breath back, let the muscles in his legs recover. Then he would return as fast as he could back to the ferry point. It was mostly downhill. There would be time to strip down and take a swim to cool off before the boat came. Alarmingly he found that his legs had unknowingly carried him nearer to the temple. He was standing amongst the old men's flowers.

Movement in the trees surrounding the temple shattered Nigel's reverie. The scurrying might have been the old men, hidden in the undergrowth. Nigel's logic was eroded as something ran clattering with great speed though the rhododendrons and magnolias towering behind the temple wall. As whatever it was ran, a piercing squeal sliced the air and Nigel fell back in fright. A disgusting odour of animal faeces wafted into his nostrils.

There were further thumps and hidden movements. Nigel stood and took a wary step backwards, terrified that some dangerous animal was lurking nearby, though some element of common sense told him it must be Alan having a little joke at his expense. Another squeal rose up, followed by a resonant grunt. Nigel's heart laboured, struggling through upwelling dread and he turned to run.

There was a russet streak across the path ahead of him and he recognized what had made the noises. A pig... no, more primitive than that... a wild boar. He realised that to return he would have to cross the path the animal had taken. If he made a run for it... it was worth a try if he wasn't to miss the boat. A boar might be dangerous, but wouldn't it be more afraid of him? Alan could take his own chances.

He dashed away from the portico, scattering some of the flowers, revealing underneath them the desiccated remains of many previous offerings. Then he came to an abrupt stop as another of the animals lumbered out of the undergrowth. It was definitely a wild boar, ugly-looking tusks and all. But how come it had the remains of a tee shirt draped around its neck? With horror Nigel remembered the other tourists. If the Italians had made it to the temple before he had, then so too had the holidaymakers. He did not see any blood on the garment, but then that didn't mean a thing. As the boar scuttled away on the other side of the path Nigel could only imagine what horror had befallen the owner of the shirt.

As he re-thought his escape plan and came up with nothing hopeful, Nigel saw another boar emerge from the trees. This monster was even bigger and more repulsive than the others. That it had Alan's camera strung around its neck neither confirmed nor denied his hypothesis that the herd were man-killers. It was when the animal turned its head and stared without blinking at Nigel, that he couldn't swallow the awful notion that suggested itself. Frozen to the spot, he had time to observe that the boar's eyes were wide with the same cast of terror that he imagined his own were. They were the agonized eyes of prey in the claws of the predator. More terribly, they were not the eyes of an animal at all, but *human* eyes, and the stark stare was brimming with the trauma of an appalling transformation.

Then the creature was gone and Nigel began his run for the ferry, his trance broken at last.

He expected – hoped – to see the Italians in

their old, dusty suits, waiting at the jetty and chatting amiably, their conversation muted by the seriousness of their mission. Nigel judged that their trip to the temple was a regular obligation. It might be an old tradition whose meaning was lost long ago. A bit of folklore. As Nigel's feet heavily tramped the path, he dismissed such folklore frippery. What he'd seen – the carpet of dead flowers at the temple – was an oft-repeated ritual to appease someone. A deity that existed in ancient times, back to the Etruscans or even to the Greeks, the goddess of the temple. Superstitions do not easily pass away when their rituals are not mere outdated idolatry. The Italians were re-enacting a ritual, one that afforded them protection; one that perhaps only the menfolk might otherwise fear. He didn't dwell on the fact that neither the other tourists nor Alan were supplicants to the goddess.

He did wonder about the beautiful Gabriella and her baleful eyes, but did not allow his imagination to run away with him too much.

Nigel concluded that if he made it to the boat and saw the old men, he, at least, would be saved. He did not expect to see those other holidaymakers or his companion ever again. That swine Alan might have shagged Tricia, but it no longer mattered. In fact, he was the only passenger returning to Bellagio on the last ferry of the week.

Whatever Gabriella and the old men were doing on the island was a matter for them, but he could guess what it might involve. His relationship with Tricia outlasted the holiday, but not by much. Who could say whether their parting had anything to do with his brief association with Alan?

And when he got home, he thought to look up those last strange words Gabriella had spoken. They were indeed Latin, as he'd guessed. 'No footsteps backwards'... there was no going back, that was the gist of it. Whether for him, Alan, or the holidaymakers, who was to say?

Agioi Apostoli, Chania, Greece

Bill never imagined he could feel so ill at ease on a summer holiday. There were so many abandoned, boarded up and half-completed buildings. Was this a new phenomenon, or had Crete always been like this? Bill tried to marshal the memories of his first holiday here in 1992, which was a goodly number of years before he and Cicely retired. Even the wild places looked unfinished, he thought, as if Zeus was about to descend with his gigantic dustpan and brush to sweep up all the rubble from the mountains and olive groves. The Sea of Crete still glistened in the Aegean light as it had always done, and the sand was not too silvery pale or too muddy dark; just right, soft in texture and cool in the morning. Bill hoped, as he gazed from his sun bed, and watched the gentle water lapping the nearby island of Agios Theodoros, that, with the glorious weather, his sense of dislocation and disquiet might be dispelled.

West of Chania the urban sprawl stretched along the ribbon of coast to Agia Apostoli, where Bill and Cicely were staying, and further on to where the big spa hotels and resorts dominated the beach-fronts of Aghia Marina, along with whole streets of tavernas and bars. Tourism was big business, but Bill was happy that their chosen location was quieter and relatively less commercialised. But this wasn't merely a summer holiday for him. He was here for another reason. The package of documents bought at the car boot sale a few months ago was what drew him to this part of Crete. It was a little mystery to be investigated, and he liked little mysteries. He particularly liked those obscure, ancient Greek myths and legends.

Cicely was happy to return to Crete for this year's holiday and she was very happy to go west, to a different part of the island than they had visited before. That tied in nicely with what was in the papers Bill had obtained, and which he had brought with him.

~

Bill had noticed the batch of documents at Ketch's car boot one Saturday morning. Cicely liked to mooch around for knick-knacks and antique ornaments for the garden; he could manage quite well without wandering round and round trestle tables all day, also without the smell from the hot-dog concession stand. But, on a table piled with second-hand books, old magazines, postcards, LPs and CDs, he came across a curious packet. It was a manila foolscap-size document wallet; an old, very dog-eared one. The sort with a button string fastening, the type he'd seen mouldering in ancient stationery cupboards, when he'd worked in the civil service, along with such other outmoded items as treasury tags, fish glue and sticks of sealing wax.

On the front of the wallet was a gummed label on which was typed "William", his namesake, which had immediately drawn him to it, as if it had been personally addressed to him. The label was stuck on over the printed text: "H.M. Stationery Office", above the HSMO crown symbol. Someone had also written

"Crete" in blue crayon across one corner. The wallet, which he could feel contained several documents, intrigued him since Greece had been one of his favourite destinations, so he bought it, contents unseen, for five pounds.

Back at home that evening, with Cicely off at one of her bowls meetings, Bill poured himself a glass of red wine, put Mike Westbrook's *Blake* on the stereo and carefully unwound the string securing the wallet. Shafts of sunlight from the slowly setting summer sun crossed through the windows and highlighted the off-white, dog-eared object. Trying to withhold any anticipation of 'wonderful things', he carefully folded back the opening flap and drew out a wad of papers, enclosed within a folded sheet of creased brown wrapping-paper.

He felt a tingle run up his arm and through his whole body, even into his groin, as he laid the contents on his lap. Butterflies in his stomach, a nervous twitch, a tingle of unease even, feelings slightly odd assailed him all at once. Trepidation at what? he wondered.

The contents were a few letters, several black and white photographs and a hand-drawn map. He imagined that disappointment was sure to follow, but he began to peruse the contents in order. The first was an envelope, addressed to a Professor Wellman at an address in Oswestry. On the envelope was a date-stamped Greek airmail postage stamp, purple-tinted, depicting Icarus and his father Daedalus. The letter was still inside the envelope, folded into four, and Bill carefully opened the fragile tissue-like paper and began to read. It was headed on the right-hand side: "Maleme, 1939". The letter had been written with what Bill assumed to be a simple ink pen, the sort he remembered from his school days. Dip the nib into the blue ink, start to write and blotches of ink-stain would inevitably follow.

Dear Professor,

I have found the small tholos tomb you mentioned to me, close to the location you gave me near Kato Daratso (photographs enclosed). I have drawn a map (pretty crude and not to scale) that gives a fairly precise location in relation to the village and surroundings, which I enclose with this letter.

As you can see from the photographs, the area of ground encompassing the tomb ruins rises from a donkey trail, up to the wooded foothills of Kidonia. The area is surrounded by olive groves, with a simple stone hut nearby, used by the olive harvesters during the autumn. The coast and the village are a mere mile and a half away, yet at the tomb I feel completely isolated. It is a lonely place, Professor.

Anyway, there are several layers of stones left standing (measuring five feet in height), forming a circle with a well-preserved entrance and lintel, and you can detect the beehive shape it would once have formed. Early Minoan, as you guessed. There is some evidence of the stone-lined walkway leading to the entrance, but most of this is either buried or has been robbed out. See the second photograph.

The site is well preserved considering it is in such an exposed area. I ducked under the lintel and entered the circular area to take more photographs inside. Unfortunately none of these developed; they are strangely fogged and there would be no point in sending them to you. I will try again next time I visit the tomb.

Once inside the tomb I had a search in case there were any artefacts left lying, but there was nothing amongst the herbs and grasses growing within the walls. A proper excavation would reveal anything of significance. I stayed to take several photographs, but have to confess a certain feeling of nausea while I worked. Probably the heat of the day as there was no shade. Then as I turned to leave, I could have sworn that I saw a shadow of someone exiting under the lintel! I called out, but there was no reply. When I too left the confines of the tomb, there was no one near. A very odd experience. It was probably a goatherd. It's what came to mind, because the smell of goats was quite strong in the tomb area. Even after I returned to Maleme I had that smell in my nostrils and – the sensation of something attached to me. If you can imagine an invisible goat pelt on your back, you would have some idea of it. Quite unpleasant for a while.

Well, for now I'll await your next letter and meanwhile see what else I can glean about the tomb.

Yours sincerely,
Benjamin.

It was Bill's intention to seek out the tholos, which he hoped was still in situ after some seventy-five years. He had that hand-drawn map of course, though Kato Daratso would have changed beyond recognition since Benjamin, the friend, colleague or student of the professor, had been there. While he lay on the beach, he contemplated a little exploration the following morning. Cicely had booked a foot fish spa and whatever other things women had done to them at these glamour boutiques.

"Cis?" he said.

"Mmm?" She was face down on the sun bed, the pale skin of her legs and arms eager to soak up the sun.

"How long will you be at the salon tomorrow?" He sat up, bringing his torso into the shade of the beach umbrella.

"Oh, I don't know, probably all morning. Will you find something to do? Don't tell me, I know – that grubby folder. You want to tread in its footsteps." She turned and raised her sunglasses and gave Bill a doubtful look.

Bill smiled. "Yes, it's a bit of history. It's one thing to check out the local archaeological museum, but entirely something else when you've got documents and a genuine mystery to investigate."

"Well perhaps." Cicely smirked. "Or perhaps you're trying to re-create a profession you were never able to aspire to."

"Not at all, Cis. It's just *interesting*."

He was about to apply some additional suntan cream when his wife said, "Shall we have elevenses?"

Later, in the beach taverna, Cicely ordered a gin and tonic and he an ouzo. The drinks came with a little bowl of olives and some crisps. Cicely began to investigate the contents of her beach bag while Bill slid the old folder out of his satchel and laid out its contents on the table.

"You know it's becoming an obsession," Cicely commented as she popped an olive into her mouth.

"Perhaps Benjamin thought so too," Bill said. "But the professor believed he was on to some significant discoveries."

"Who's Benjamin?" she asked while concentrating again on the contents of her bag.

"The letter writer." He waved a sheet of quarto paper at her. "Shall I read this one to you?"

"I'd rather you didn't," Cicely answered as she found and began to apply some lipstick.

"Spikey!"

"I'm not being spikey, Bill, just realistic." It had become a sort of term of endearment. He would say "Spikey" and Cicely, if she was in a good mood, would often reply "Spokey" as if to put a spoke in his wheel. This short and snappy repartee had been part of their married life almost from the start.

Bill sipped his ouzo, removed his sunglasses and began to re-read the second document in the folder, another letter from Benjamin. As he cast his eye over the date, he thought it likely, very likely in fact, that there were a number of 'missing' letters from Benjamin; ones that the professor had not seen fit to keep.

Maleme, 1940.

Dear Professor,

The Drosoulites you mentioned in your last letter are a more modern legend from the south of the island. And I am sure you are aware of their provenance as so-called visions of an army that fought at the battle of Frangokastello, where the Greeks were massacred by the besieging Turks, in the 17th century.

You theorise that these visions actually date from an earlier time, and that the Greeks reinterpreted or created this ghostly host based upon more ancient myths or legends. Personally I feel that the one theory that accounts for these human-like shadows is mirages, although I have to say that my odd experience at the tholos tomb mimics the accepted conventions of these so-called "dew-shadows": the shadow I thought I saw appeared when the sea was calm and the atmosphere humid and not long after dawn... fitting the accepted conventions perfectly.

But coincidences aside, I will do as you ask and try to find earlier examples of the legend, or similar, to attempt to fit it into your theories of the early Minoans who lived in the Chania area.

Yours,

Benjamin.

P.S. Nearly forgot to mention that I am shortly to meet with Manolis Koutselinis, an expert on Cretan folklore. He has invited me to his house for dinner and has offered to let me see his extensive library.

~

Bill stood with his back to the sea and with the coast road, Kissamou Chanion, before him. Traffic was heavy, but interspersed with short periods of quiet. A bus to Chania passed by on the opposite side. He opened out the map Benjamin had drawn and tried to make sense of it. There was a dotted line that roughly followed the shape of the coast, which Bill thought was probably this road, though it was more irregular than was shown on the modern Topo map he'd brought with him. What was accurate was the shape of the coastline. A wide, shallow bay with a small headland to the west and the larger peninsula with Aghii Apostoli church and Iguana beach beyond to the east.

He felt he was in the correct position based on the beach and headlands. Opposite him was a narrow road which led steeply upwards before turning right. On the main road either side of it was a taverna and a mini-market. The hand-drawn map was marked "donkey trail", and a dotted line snaked up into the hills marked as Kydonia. Bill noted the street signs indicating several apartments further up the road, the road that his map reading suggested had been the donkey track in the nineteen-forties. Modern development could mean his search might be fruitless, but he crossed the main road and strode up the steep incline, following what he hoped would lead him to the "tholos tomb" inscribed on the drawing in red ink.

Several hire cars were tucked into the narrow passing places on the dusty road, and apartment blocks advertised their facilities. After not too long the road turned and levelled off a little and he came to a desolate house. A single-storey property, it looked long abandoned. Its window shutters, flaking paint, were closed and the front door had a rusty iron gate fixed in front. The garden behind a low wall was overgrown with a huge olive tree. Behind the house, rising into the hills, were olive groves.

Could this have been the site of the tomb, Bill wondered? If so, the house now occupied its position and that was the end of his expedition. "Spikey" would have won the day... It had been seventy plus years since Benjamin had created his little map. And sadly, this seemed to be the exact spot indicated.

Yet he didn't want to give up quite so quickly. He removed his sun hat and wiped sweat from his brow. The air was hot and still. Cicadas buzzed in the trees, a multitude of scratching screeches that rose in a crescendo and then stopped as suddenly as they began.

Putting away the map into his rucksack, Bill was about to step over the low wall of the house when he noticed the plot of land next to it. It also had a low wall, but was topped with rusty mesh-link fencing supported by crumbling concrete pillars. It had the appearance of a garden gone back to nature. There was an orange tree in one corner and a fig draping its branches and leaves over the fence about halfway along. Old vines wove themselves through the mesh and struggled and drooped against the other wild plants that had more or less taken over completely, and which were able to stand without support.

Bill had a hunch this might be the place and he walked on, down the side of the perimeter fence, to see if he could gain access or at least see through the screen of tall grasses. Near the rear side of the garden one of the retaining posts had broken in half and taken the fencing with it, leaving a convenient opening to step through.

Without thinking he entered the garden and stood amongst grasses nearly as tall as he was.

Vines tried in vain to climb up them for support and cow parsley seed heads bloomed as big as his fist. The cicadas began their chirruping again. It occurred to Bill that he was probably trespassing. However, he must be almost unseen from the road, so any nervousness on his part could be allayed.

But Bill was excited and edgy. He began to walk carefully towards the centre of the area, sweeping away vegetation with his arms. There was a definite slope downwards and as he looked seawards there was no road to see anymore, only the pale blue sky. He was standing below the level of the concrete wall. Up to his right the olive trees climbed the hills; black nets sagged below them, waiting for the harvest.

He was hemmed in by the heat and was thinking he should really get back to the hotel when he came up against a stone doorway arch.

This is it! He almost cried out loud. He had found the tholos tomb. But why hadn't the Greek government preserved it, or at least put a notice on the fence? Kept the vegetation at bay? Perhaps the land was privately owned and the owner was responsible, but disinclined to advertise the site. Whatever the reason for its neglected state, once Bill had ducked under the opening he found to his surprise that the riotous jungle of wild plants, grasses and trees outside the tomb walls was not replicated inside.

The site was a circular space around twenty metres in diameter, with about two metres height of the remaining walls. Nothing much grew within the walls; bleached, stunted grass was all. Goats must recently have used the tomb as a resting place, for Bill could smell that they had been here.

The heat was wearing. Bill sat on one of the tumbled stones from the wall and unhitched his rucksack. He wondered what the outcome of Benjamin's researches had been, what was his history and that of his professor? The letters and pictures were tantalising, yet incomplete. Perhaps he might find out more when he and Cicely returned to England?

He opened the rucksack and slid out the old file. Straightaway he found the last of the letters and read through it again.

Maleme, May 1941.

Dear Professor,
 Time is against us I am afraid. We have been

told that the German invasion has begun and I must leave the island immediately. However, I plan to escape over the White Mountains and either team up with the Greek resistance or, failing that, negotiate the Samaria gorge and find a ship at Sfakia and return to England.

I cannot post this letter, so am entrusting it to Sgt Edwin Thompson, who has promised me that he will deliver it or post it to you when he arrives back in England.

All of the RAF 30 squadron based here at Maleme are to be evacuated to save the aircraft and crew. Sgt Thomson is the pilot of one of the Blenheims based here and I think he will be carrying much documentation that we would not want to fall into enemy hands, besides my less important correspondence! I imagine he will fly to an aerodrome in Egypt first, so this letter may be some time in arriving!

Gathering the evidence has been thwarted I fear, unless Crete survives the German onslaught. I hope that the information I have supplied thus far will prove useful. Although you asked me to seek out folk-tales from locals in the west of the island, I don't entirely see their relevance to the archaeology. There are some curious rituals performed in isolated villages and I have elaborated on some of those already. I understand that certain ancient practices pre-date recorded history, but still find it difficult to imagine that any of those I have transcribed went back even to the Bronze Age. Manolis talked about a Dionysian cult in Bronze Age Minoan Crete. He is of the opinion that there are some survivals of the rituals in secluded places on the island, at isolated tombs. I shall enclose my notes on this with this letter.

I confess I am fearful, Professor; the shadow of war is an oppression upon me, it cloaks me as if a shade hides just beyond the corner of vision, sidling beside me and intent on malice. Just listen to me, Professor! Manolis and his tales have turned me into a gibbering, gullible fool! They and the war are likely to give me nightmares until I flee this place...

When I return to Oswestry (pray for my safe journey, Professor), I hope we can discuss the research I have been undertaking and I look forward to an interim conclusion to your theories in the light of peace.

Yours, in trepidation,
Benjamin.

Bill carefully re-folded the letter along its original crease and returned it to the folder. The letter was a strange one and Bill wondered what had become of Benjamin and the professor. Why had the correspondence ended up in an HMSO document wallet? Was there a connection with the military, other than having the last letter flown out of Crete by a military plane? Bill had researched what had happened in Crete during the Second World War and had found out that the RAF did have several of the twin-engine Bristol Blenheim light bombers based at Maleme in 1941.

He looked at his watch and decided it was about time to return to town and his wife. He dialled her number on his mobile, but found that there was no signal. In any case, the smell of goats was overpowering and he needed to escape it. Packing his rucksack, Bill was aware of the heat and the stillness of the place. It had been a tomb for the dead after all, so there must be ancient atmospheres, real or imagined. Yet, as Bill headed for the entranceway, he sensed an emanation, as if the stubbled ground of the tomb's hard-packed floor was giving rise to a secretion. An invisible vapour, like the ripple of hot air in the distance, presented as a shimmering sheet of water, a mirage, but of a different kind. Bill could imagine this hallowed place being used for ancient rituals, if it was prone to generate mirages. It certainly had an aura to it, but not one that Bill found he much liked any more.

The ripple of air coalesced into a shadow that appeared to slip away under the lintel of the entrance and Bill recalled Benjamin's experience here before the war. Water and shadows. Mirages, optical illusions... Bill ducked and left the confines of the tomb ruins.

Cicely said, "You look terrible, Bill. Did you put on some sun cream, like I said?"

He'd met her on her walk back to the hotel from her foot spa. "Of course. But it's hot without any shade. And I had to do a bit of walking." As he said it, he couldn't help glancing over his shoulder. His foreshortened shadow wrinkled on the uneven pavement behind him.

"Looking for someone?" She took his arm in hers and they strode towards the hotel entrance and cool shade.

Inside the lobby, Bill shivered. Perhaps he

was beginning to get sunstroke. Goosebumps tingled on his damp back, held icily in place by his rucksack. As Cicely headed for the stairs, he shrugged the straps off his shoulders and was immediately aware of an indistinct shape behind him. He expected to see another holidaymaker as he turned, but the beginning of his smile faded as there was no one there. Yet – he tried peering over his shoulder again – there might have been something clinging to his back, as if his own shadow was trying to hide away, sneakily avoiding being seen. All of a sudden, he wished the contents of the folder had offered more information. Bill thought he might soon need to know more.

"Are you coming?" Cicely asked from the top of the first flight of stairs.

"Yes," Bill answered, confusion and sweat blistering his brow. Me *and* the other one, he whispered to himself; his lips a rictus smile. Bill's nostrils filled with a stench that was a mixture of urine and musk. Behind him something stirred, very close, cunning in its stealth. He craned his neck to see over his shoulder again, but if there was a second shadow replacing his, it was, for the moment, keeping a low profile.

Cicely tried to concentrate on the Kalooki card game she was having with three of her friends. But there was an unpleasant meaty smell coming from the kitchen, even though she hadn't cooked this evening.

"How are things going, Cis?" Jill asked her, as she shuffled the packs. Her other two companions murmured their consolations. The conversation was bound to get around to it eventually. Jill was a widow of long standing and considered herself well qualified to offer support. Cicely had been grateful for her company these past weeks.

"I'm getting there, I think." Mourning Bill had been difficult. She wanted to retort "Spokey" to his "Spikey", but he would never be there again to respond.

"What *was* he thinking..." Mary blurted out, then, "Oh, I'm sorry Cicely, I didn't mean to..."

Cicely had tried to keep the details confidential, but the state of the skin on Bill's back was a confounded mystery. "It's all right. I think his mental state wasn't good, just before..." She sank into silence. Mary might well have wallowed in the more sensational details beyond the newspaper obituaries, but at least she might keep her lips fastened, Cicely thought.

Unspoken, the card game was at an end. Her friends began to get ready to leave, with further commiserations.

"God be with you," Brenda added as Cicely waved her friends off. She nodded a thank you and, as she leaned back against the closed door, wondered if somehow Brenda knew she needed God's help.

Cicely had tried to find an answer when Bill had died, and had read through that damned folder. The newspaper cutting fluttered out after she had angrily ripped the folder open to disgorge its contents onto the dining table. It had been stuck inside, scrunched in a corner and Bill had probably never seen it. There was nothing to indicate the year, or from which newspaper it had been cut.

6th March.

Professor Richard Wellman.
Born Oswestry, 18th June 1871.
Richard Wellman was well known for his studies of the Minoan civilisations of Crete. His

books include two on early and late Minoan peoples and a third on the folklore of ancient Greece. In later life he lost favour with academia because of his views on spirituality and folklore.

The professor was well known locally for his eccentricity, which extended to his garden. This he had adorned with Greek statuary. One carved figure, named by the local neighbours "The Green Man", was probably an interpretation of Dionysus.

Professor Wellman was found dead near the statue, shirtless and with scarring upon his shoulders. The coroner recorded his death the result of heart failure and noted that the disfigurement was self-inflicted.

The remarkable coincidence is that one of the professor's former students, Benjamin Biddell, who also died recently of a heart attack, was found with similar lacerations on his back. The coroner in this case said that he had been whipping himself with what was probably a length of barbed wire. It is the conclusion of this writer that both men had suffered some type of psychotic episode, which hastened their deaths.

Cicely sipped at her glass of white wine as she listened to the engine of her friends' car start up outside. Silence eventually filled the house.

She glanced over at the photograph of Bill on the chimney breast and imagined she saw a shadow pass across it. Cicely shivered. "Someone has stepped on my grave," she whispered. Although it wasn't particularly warm inside the house, she opened a window for ventilation. The smell, she thought. A bit of fresh air should get rid of it.

Also by David A. Sutton:

Collections

Voices from Shadow (Shadow Publishing, 1994)
Clinically Dead & Other Tales of the Supernatural (Crowswing Books, 2006)
Dead Water and Other Weird Tales (The Alchemy Press, 2015)

Chapbooks

The Fisherman (Gothic Press, 2007)

As Editor

New Writings in Horror and the Supernatural (Sphere, 1971)
New Writings in Horror and the Supernatural #2 (Sphere, 1972)
The Satyr's Head and Other Tales of Terror (Corgi, 1975)
The Best Horror from Fantasy Tales (Robinson, 1988, with Stephen Jones)
Dark Voices 2 (Pan, 1990, with Stephen Jones)
Dark Voices 3 (Pan, 1991, with Stephen Jones)
Dark Voices 4 (Pan, 1992, with Stephen Jones)
Dark Voices 5 (Pan, 1993, with Stephen Jones)
Dark Voices 6 (Pan, 1994, with Stephen Jones)

The Anthology of Fantasy & the Supernatural (Tiger Books International, 1994, with Stephen Jones)
Dark Terrors (Gollancz, 1995, with Stephen Jones)
Dark Terrors 2 (Gollancz, 1996, with Stephen Jones)
The Giant Book of Fantasy Tales (The Book Company, 1996, with Stephen Jones)
Dark Terrors 3 (Gollancz, 1997, with Stephen Jones)
Dark Terrors 4 (Gollancz, 1998, with Stephen Jones)
Dark Terrors 5 (Gollancz, 2000, with Stephen Jones)
Phantoms of Venice (Shadow Publishing, 2001)
Dark Terrors 6 (Gollancz, 2002, with Stephen Jones)
Houses on the Borderland (The British Fantasy Society, 2008)
Horror! Under the Tombstone: Stories from the Deathly Realm (Shadow Publishing, 2013)
Horror on the High Seas: Classic Weird Sea Tales (Shadow Publishing, 2014)
Darker Terrors (Spectral Press, 2015, with Stephen Jones)

Non-Fiction

*On the Fringe for Thirty Years: A History of Horror
in the British Small Press* (Shadow Publishing,
2000)

*Now available and forthcoming from
Black Shuck Shadows:*

Shadows 1 – The Spirits of Christmas
by Paul Kane

Shadows 2 – Tales of New Mexico
by Joseph D'Lacey

Shadows 3 – Unquiet Waters
by Thana Niveau

Shadows 4 – The Life Cycle
by Paul Kane

Shadows 5 – The Death of Boys
by Gary Fry

Shadows 6 – Broken on the Inside
by Phil Sloman

Shadows 7 – The Martledge Variations
by Simon Kurt Unsworth

Shadows 8 – Singing Back the Dark
by Simon Bestwick

blackshuckbooks.co.uk/shadows